Also by Bryon Williams

The Grumpy Old Withered of Oz

The Twilight Escort Agency

Tourist from the Light

The Burning Boy

The Reluctant Psychic

Naked Warrior

A Light at the End

The Psychic Spy

Not in the Public Interest

Code name "Millicent"

The Cat Intelligence Agent
Who Came Out Of The Cold

A novel
by Bryon Williams

Code Name "Millicent"

The Cat Intelligence Agent Who Came Out Of The Cold

Copyright BRYON WILLIAMS 2010

Email: bryonwilliams@tpg.com.au

ISBN: 978-0-6484238-5-0

Subject: Fantasy-Humour – Fiction – Crime

All rights reserved

No part of this book may be reproduced in any form, by photocopying or by any electronic or mechanical means, including information storage or retrieval systems, without permission in writing from the copyright owner and the publisher of this book.

This book is a work of fiction and any resemblance to any persons (or animals) living or dead is purely coincidental.

The author asserts all moral rights.

Copyright Cover Design – Bryon Williams, Helen Morgan and Emma Gloede

Dedication

This book is dedicated to all cat lovers in the world who flood the internet with stories and pictures of cats. You know who you are.
I must also add a dedication to my Oriental Shorthair cat, Medici Crocodile Hunter, AKA Rocky, who ruled my life for twenty years.

Acknowledgements

This book would not have been possible without the incredibly helpful assistance of my late wife, Marie, for her proofreading and unbiased critical appraisal; Julie Winzar, my editor, who is a delight to work with, for her friendship, ability and understanding; and to the lovely Helen Morgan and Emma Gloede whose technical assistance, friendship and support in bringing this all together was invaluable. Thank you, guys!

Introduction

Her last assignment had been a bad experience. She had been sent to freezing cold Dunedin in the south island of New Zealand as support for another agent, Kitty – a dumb code name for a cat, she considered – who was a rather ugly, hairless Sphinx with huge brown eyes set in a wedge-shaped head. Her almost naked skin fell in unattractive folds that belied her age. She looked more like a four-footed, ninety-year-old pole dancer. She was sent to work undercover, or in her case, being a sleeper mostly, 'under the covers,' with a particularly vicious gang called The Mongrels. Kitty should have realised, being dogs, she would have to take extreme precautions.

Typical of her breed, she was energetic, mischievous, a bit of a clown and frankly, not too bright. Kitty was only recruited as an agent because she had friends in high places, a favoured position for cats. Little did she know the gang was on to her and had started lacing her Whiskas with crushed amphetamines. Kitty inevitably got hooked and turned. Unbeknown to Headquarters, she had become a double agent and the information she was sending back was badly compromised.

Her partner, an Oriental Shorthair code-named Mana, meaning 'persistence' in Thai, tried desperately to rehabilitate her but to no avail; she was past the rehab stage. Kitty was stoned out of her brain one night and acting even sillier than usual, and Mana was trying to debrief her when The Mongrels attacked. The two agents were captured, beaten and tortured mercilessly, and then kidnapped or, I suppose, in their case, cat-napped.

The Mongrels stuffed them into the saddle bag of a motorcycle with the intention of throwing them down a deep crevasse or dumping them in the river – trying to flush them down a toilet having failed – but fortunately, the saddle bag flap was carelessly left unbuckled and Mana managed to grab Kitty by the scruff of the neck and jump, pushing the flap up to escape, with Kitty hanging from her mouth like a sagging, wrinkled piece of untanned leather.

Mana suffered dreadful trauma from the ordeal, both mental and physical, but poor Kitty didn't make it; her lifeless body was wrapped around the pole of a roadside sign giving directions to Queenstown, looking like some wet chamois that someone had carelessly thrown from a passing car. It was only due to Mana's remarkable strength and determination that she managed to escape by hitching a ride on a passing snow plough and then snowboarding to a safe-house where she was picked up by one of the Agency's choppers and flown to safety.

But the experience had left an indelible mark on her psyche and she was relieved of duty for several months while she recovered in an Agency cat-house. With her failure to complete her assignment and the loss of her partner, for which she blamed herself, she went into a deep decline and hit the Vasse Felix dry red like it was mother's milk. At this low point in her career she decided to quit the Agency and retire, but her skills and experience in the field were far too valuable for the Agency to ignore. After suffering severe deprivation, she was eventually dried out and after undergoing intense physical and psychological rehabilitation sessions, she was finally persuaded back into the field.

Now she was fully recovered and it was time to get back to work.

Chapter 1

Mana's code name now was changed to Millicent; well, at least that was the name encoded on the microchip embedded in the muscle of her left shoulder. Her pedigree name was actually Princess Srirasmi, named after the Thai Crown Prince's consort. Originally, of course, she claimed her pedigree could be traced right back to Siam's King Buddha Yodfa Chulaloke, founder of the Chakri Dynasty in the late eighteenth century. But of course all of this back-ground information was now classified and stored in the depths of the official archives under the strict classification of 'Top Secret – On a Need to Know Basis Only.'

The old Siamese king was a great cat fancier and delighted in the company of the large number of Siamese cats he kept in the palace as his personal companions. He loved their elegance, their smooth velvety coats, their amazing, brilliant blue eyes and the way they slunk through the palace and throne room. And of course they showed such intelligence, loyalty, love and trust and could always be relied on to ferret out intrigues and gossip around the palace. So, with that heritage, it was a foregone conclusion that Millicent would eventually be recruited as a secret agent for the CIA: the Cat Intelligence Agency.

She received her assignments from the CIA headquarters in Canberra mostly by email. We all know how cats love to sit on computer keyboards but we never expect them to be actually typing or corresponding by email. It's just another clever ruse to make us think they're sleeping when actually they are merely biding their time until we leave the office or the house and then it's back to their secretive inter-office plotting and scheming.

It's just part of their nature to conceal their dubious intentions from their so-called owners, who, unknowingly, are really considered 'servants'. They will never come when they are called, of course, unless it is time for their dinner or they insist on being let out. They graciously allow us to fuss over them and feed them tasty morsels, pet and stroke them, install pet doors for their convenience and freedom of movement, clean their litter trays constantly after every use, much like the servants of the Forbidden City in Peking were called upon to do for the old Chinese Emperors; and they even allow us to share our beds with them!

In return they leap onto our laps, curling themselves into soft, comforting, fluffy balls and purr – very loudly! They allow us to stroke them and rub their ears and if we don't they nudge us with their nose until we do. This is not for our benefit of course, but for theirs. They are sublimely content. But if you displease them in any way, such as buying the wrong food, or forgetting to refresh their water bowl, or not cleaning their litter tray on demand, or accidentally locking the pet door, there is hell to pay and they berate you loudly and stridently until you come to heel.

This is particularly true of the Siamese breed of which Millicent, as an Oriental Shorthair, ebony-tipped tabby, is undeniably a descendant. I'm not quite sure how the breed came about but I suspect there was the odd dalliance between the regal Siamese and the occasional street moggie they encountered on their nightly forays into the seedier side of Siam. Sometimes this resulted in a slight physical chromosome defect and the offspring may be born with pale jade-green eyes, different fur colours – sometimes a solid colour or tabby striped or even ginger, but their nature will always remain regal and aloof. These abnormalities do occur even in the strictest, most well-bred, royal social circles of today, I suspect. Since as late as 1977, the result of these nefarious encounters is now recognised as a breed of its own. Oriental Shorthairs are now given their rightful place amongst the superior class of feline society.

Apart from the email correspondence capability, Millicent also has another secret silicone chip inserted at the base of her skull, which is fitted with GPS and a microscopic microphone, recorder and speaker system. This is why sometimes she appears to be just sitting idly in the warm sun, gazing out into the middle distance, when actually she is receiving instructions from headquarters, or conversing with her collaborators, or being advised of the latest troop movements or terrorist plots. It is then that you will see her escape swiftly through the pet flap and disappear into the undergrowth, ostensibly to hunt for lizards or insects, when she is actually radioing back her report on the current assignment or receiving instructions on the latest terrorist situation.

Millicent was certainly a beautiful creature, though some insensitive humans, mainly dog lovers, considered her rather weird looking for a cat. But in truth she was an absolute *femme fatale* with a long sleek body, fine legs, slender feet with elegant toes reminiscent of a concert pianist's hands, topped with long pointed claws, and the sensual stride of a catwalk model. Her fur was satin soft in a pale taupe shade with darker patches on her back and matching subtle stripes on her seductive hips and serpent tail. She had a delightful breastplate and stomach of soft cream fur that invited stroking, but if one dared, she would lash out with her claws or on occasion, deliver a nip from her strong, sharp, white teeth to discourage any unwanted familiarity. Her ears were large, pointed and beautifully formed and stood straight out from her noble head like wings. At a sign of impending danger, like the unappreciated attention of children, she could fold them back much like the wings of a F111 fighter plane. That was a warning sign which, if ignored, was at your own peril. Her face narrowed to a petite, dark brown, pointed nose and soft, cream, furry chin giving her head a triangular or wedged-shaped appearance.

Her forehead was also distinctively striped above long, proud whiskers, which enabled her to judge the size of an aperture she had to pass through. Her slanted, oriental eyes were a shining, pale jade green and totally inscrutable. One never could tell what she was thinking and had to rely on her body language and the pitch of her strident yell for any sort of indication. To lesser humans this was confusing to say the least.

Secretly, Millicent was amused when overhearing the oft-made statement that 'cats have nine lives'. She, of course, knew better. She had had many incarnations stretching back to long before the Egyptian dynasties. In fact, she considered herself a direct descendant of Queen Bastet, the Egyptian cat goddess. She had always decided to return to the earthly plane as a cat. Why would she decide otherwise?

Cats were privileged creatures set aside from other animals, particularly the domesticated variety, and she would certainly not entertain the notion of coming back as a human. Humans, on the whole, were most unreliable; cruel, greedy, self-serving, corruptible, intolerant and prone to war and other atrocities. They had always shown these tendencies and, no doubt, always would. It was a part of their nature and, she assumed, part of their soul's development.

She believed in strong self-defence in the case of attack, of course, and pity the animal that dared stray into her territory or threaten her family or staff. Otherwise she believed in 'live and let live', aside from the odd hunting foray for mice or insects and the occasional stupid bird or lizard which happened by, or tried to run and hide to evade her attention. But hunting was entirely for the game and sustenance and besides, she knew that the soul of the hapless meal would quickly return to the Great Universal power to be reborn again in yet another body as was the order of all living things. If only humans would avail themselves of this basic cosmic truth there would not be the amount of intolerance, confrontation, senseless killing and suffering in their world.

But Millicent had learned that this would never happen as humans believed themselves superior to all living things and practised denial of cosmic truth, self-absorption and the belief that everyone should think and believe as they do. She had long learned of their moral frailty and adjusted to their odd behaviour, learning to work within their framework whilst still maintaining her advanced intellect and age-old spiritual wisdom.

Millicent had been recruited into the CIA by a particularly charming and, she must admit, devilishly attractive tom-cat who went by the name, although obviously an alias, of Tom. For the first few years she had always deferred to him as Mr Cat, but now, after the many exciting and dangerous assignments and adventures they had shared together, they had developed a great sense of trust and respect for each other and he had generously suggested she call him by his first name, Tom.

Tom was an amber-eyed Tawny Somali, older and much tougher than she, and on many occasions he had miraculously appeared in the nick of time to save her from life-threatening situations. They had bravely fought side by side to overcome adversaries and prevail.

But this time she was far from the support of her protector and had been sent north to the upper Northern Rivers region of New South Wales to a little town called Nimbin. At least she was far removed from the cold and snow of New Zealand's south island. Nimbin had become a hippy destination for the 'Love and Peace' brigade of the sixties and within a short time had developed a reputation for the use, growing, harvesting, selling and distribution of marijuana.

Understandably, the locals were happy and content to live a life of naturalist freedom in the beautiful bushland setting away from the rigors of careers, commercialism, overcrowding and crime. For a time it had remained quaint and somewhat local in its dope operations but, as usual, eventually crime bosses recognised the potential to feed their greed and increase their bank balances and moved in to dominate the operation. The local growers and suppliers were unfortunately too stoned to realise the danger that was about to be visited upon them and got on with their nudity, free love and macrobiotic existence. But eventually the drug trade, as it had become, drew the attention of the news and gossip-hungry media, which, in turn, prompted the vote-conscious politicians, who saw themselves as moral arbiters, and the law was forced to intervene.

That is how the invincible Millicent became involved. Tom had met her in the bushes behind Parliament House and issued her with her instructions. She was to investigate the extent of the drug trade and gather intelligence which she would relate back to the Agency. She was to be flown into Nimbin by an agency helicopter, parachute into the surrounding bush during the night, reconnoitre the area, find a suitable hideout, infiltrate one of the local residences and become one of the family. Once safely ensconced, she would assume her usual control over the owners and by her cunning, guile and deception, gain their love, trust and protection, and her real task could begin.

She was also instructed to seek out and enlist reliable informers who could be coerced into assisting in her operation. She would then gather intelligence of the criminal activities in the area and pass this sensitive information on to Tom via email, if possible, or by the protected radio channel embedded in her microchip, and await further instructions.

This was a daunting task for Millicent as she had never been required to operate as a loner without close backup in the target area and she had never been sent on an assignment so far north where the heat could be interminable. She was a cold-climate operator and more of a sophisticated city girl with little experience of the bush and alternative living or possibly drugged-up country folk. She'd seen her share of action with the tough city gangs and boys of the hood in the past and, apart from her last unfortunate experience, had escaped relatively unharmed; but this was new territory and she had no idea quite what to expect.

She took this as a sign of confidence from Tom and the Agency and deep down she was thrilled to be given the opportunity once again to show her true mettle in recruiting her own people and gathering valuable intelligence without having to bring in the 'big guns' unless absolutely necessary. She had been well trained in karate and all the martial arts and knew how to take care of herself but there was always the danger of the unexpected in foreign territory and this aspect added a certain thrill to the venture.

Chapter 2

On the night of the flight she met with Butch, the model helicopter pilot. He was a well-built, middle-aged, tough-looking tabby character, she suspected of ordinary alley-cat heritage, with several scars, scratch marks and patches of missing fur that hinted at a life of hard knocks. But he knew his trade and she felt a strong confidence in his ability to get her safely to her destination.

She'd been issued her equipment which, of course, included the usual cyanide death pill in the case of capture and torture, and a vacuum pack of kitty litter and dried cat food emergency rations which she carried in a waterproof satchel around her neck. She secretly slipped in a bunch of catnip as a stress relief medication and a nail file to sharpen her claws if a scratching post was not available in her new location but she felt sure a nice piece of tree bark would be readily available in the bush and she was prepared to rough it.

She'd also been presented with a rather beautiful black, metal-impregnated, suede collar studded with diamantes, and a pendant engraved with her code name. Behind one of the diamantes was a secret compartment which held the emergency death pill. The diamantes also acted as an excellent reflector or Morse code signal if the need arose.

At the appointed map co-ordinates, Butch gave her the claw-up signal and she jumped into the cool inky blackness. She was not afraid of heights of course, but the breeze of the descent ruffled her fur which she hated. However, this was a small price to pay for the success of the mission. Attached to her parachute, fashioned from a large green and brown, camouflage- patterned silk handkerchief, she gently floated down to the small bush clearing that had been chosen for her landing. The trees and long grass encircled the clearing in blackness with not a light to be seen except for the soft illumination from the pale silver moon hidden partly by dark rain clouds.

True to her training, she hit the soft ground, rolled onto her back and looked up into the net of sparkling stars and scattered cloud that covered the sky. But Butch and the chopper were gone leaving only the softest whine and the sound of the receding rotor blades. She was totally alone in the surrounding darkness.

She rolled onto her stomach and lay very still, listening. But the only sounds that came to her highly sensitive ears were those of cicadas and other insects and in the far distance a dog barking: Must keep an eye out for that. A dog bark could betray her position and invite unfriendly investigation, which would necessitate a quick leap and hasty climb up into a tree to hide amongst the branches until the enemy had passed by.

When she was certain her arrival had not been detected, she quickly pushed the release button of her chute with her paw and shrugged off the harness. She then dug a deep hole in the soft ground into which she pushed the parachute. The excitement and tension of the jump caused a familiar tightening of her bladder so she took the opportunity to relieve herself in the hole before quickly covering it with the soil she had scraped out with her paws. She turned and sniffed the area to ensure there were no telltale signs of her presence and satisfied, crept stealthily into the bush.

Climbing a nearby tree to get her bearings, Millicent saw in the distance the lights of the town and carefully climbed back down and headed towards them, her eyes and ears on full alert. The dog barked again, this time closer. Perhaps he had caught her scent. She stopped to evaluate the direction from which the bark came and made a wide berth away from the foe.

She carefully explored many residences but was dissuaded by growling or barking dogs, which necessitated a hasty retreat. She also met many other cats on their nightly prowl and social gatherings. There were the inevitable confrontations but with her intense psychological training, which she'd received from the Agency experts, she was able to talk her way out of any physical attack while remaining in total control of the situation. The local feline population were, on the whole, a rather submissive lot, obviously inbred and intellectually inferior to Millicent, and lacked the physical, mental and psychological training she had undergone. This of course gave her a distinct edge.

After the expected initial hostility displayed by the locals concerning the usual territorial rights, tests of combat and the ensuing cacophony of yells followed by the inevitable projectiles being thrown at the screeching combatants by the annoyed inhabitants of the surrounding area, it was soon clear that Millicent was not a female to be trifled with and eventually elicited grudging respect, or at least, tolerance.

Presently she came to a darkened human accommodation and quietly reconnoitred the area. It appeared to be some sort of small farm with rows of crops growing in a fenced-off area at the rear of the property. The garden area was well maintained with lots of shrubs and flowers. An old weather-beaten utility truck stood sentinel in the front yard close to a gravel path, which led to a set of three steps and a marine-varnished verandah and a recently painted, dark green wooden door with a polished brass doorknob. A wheat-coloured, coarse woven doormat with a stencilled 'Welcome' greeting printed on it, lay in front of the door for visitors. – Or perhaps cats?

She crept up onto the verandah and sniffed the area for a sign of pets, noting the familiar odour of sprayed territorial borders. At that moment she heard a soft growl behind her and quickly turned, immediately adopting the *kamae* karate defensive posture, her green eyes searching for the hostile opponent. On the window ledge above her in the dominant position, she observed an old grey moggie, obviously part Persian or some other hairy cross breed. Her straggly fur stood on end and her thin lips were pulled back in a show of unwelcoming disapproval, displaying three yellowing teeth and a lot of slightly discoloured gum. Her ears were tattered and one blue eye was partly closed from old wounds. From her pose Millicent deduced that this would-be opponent was suffering from arthritis and hence was hardly a threat. On the whole she had the rather comical appearance of a badly made duster.

Millicent relaxed and sat sedately, all four paws placed together, head held high, her tail neatly curled around to sit in the fold of her hip bone.

'Oh, hi,' she purred in a friendly manner, 'I'm Millicent, and you are …?'

'Bertha,' the old cat growled, 'and what would you be doing up here in my territory, young lady?'

'Sorry,' said Millicent in an apologetic tone. 'You see, I'm new in the area and I don't quite know my way around yet.'

'Where you from?' Bertha inquired warily. 'I don't remember seeing you around the place. But I don't get around much anymore – old and arthritic and only one good eye. But I can still look after meself,' she added warningly in case this intruder thought she was a pushover.

'Oh, I can see that,' Millicent said in an attempt to placate her. 'Blue Knob. I've just trekked in from Blue Knob.'

'Mmmm, Blue Knob,' replied Bertha with the hint of surprise in her voice. 'That's quite a trek.'

'You can say that again,' Millicent smiled.

Yes, cats can smile; they are not in the least agelastic – incapable of smiling or laughing. They just do not approve of smiling and laughing in front of humans. It's best to remain inscrutable; it just makes them appear more mysterious. Many was the time that Millicent had a good old laugh with her comrades; rolling around the ground in apparent hysterics. But now was not the time to laugh when faced with a funny-looking, grey, overweight, mixed-breed matron of a cat with arthritis and, Millicent suspected, a bad case of halitosis.

'I'm pretty exhausted,' she admitted. 'I don't suppose you have a bowl of water you'd allow me to share?'

'Later,' said Bertha, curtly. 'Firstly, what brings you to these parts, *Ms Millicent*?' She pronounced the name almost patronisingly.

Millicent crouched down in what she hoped was a subservient pose and went into her cover story. 'Well, my carers decided to move to Murwillumbah – a work-related move – and I overheard them saying their new place wasn't big enough to swing a cat around in and pets weren't allowed anyway so they'd have to take me back to the breeder where they got me. Well, there was no way I was going back there. They used to keep me caged up and wash and preen me in a most undignified manner, clip and polish my claws, and put me in cat shows all over the country! Mind you,' she continued, feigning modesty, 'I was a Gold Medallist in my class but I really hated being shown off like that. It was so demeaning.'

'I can imagine,' agreed Bertha, somewhat enviously, 'but surely there were perks that went with the title – publicity, pictures in the newspapers ... fish to eat whenever you wanted ...?'

'Not for me,' Millicent replied, shaking her head dismissively. 'I can't stand fish anyway. Oh, my so-called carers got the cups, medals and ribbons, walls and cases of them, but I was treated as an object; no love and affection or freedom – just a prize to show and own. And my cage didn't even have a view!

'Anyway,' she continued, 'I accidentally picked up an infection at one of their blasted cat shows which turned rather nasty and I finished up at the local vet's with,' she paused dramatically and lowered her voice, 'female problems.'

Bertha was transfixed by Millicent's story and her one good eye enlarged to the size of a pet bowl. 'You weren't …?' She left the word unspoken.

Millicent nodded pathetically. 'Yes, I was … neutered. Never again to have kittens of my own to play with and hear the gentle mewing and patter of little paws around my cage.'

Bertha choked back a sob.

'But, on the positive side, I wasn't allowed to be shown again either. I was no longer a … breeder, you see. So, after the operation I was offered for sale. It was either that or the pound, I heard. This lovely young couple from Blue Knob arrived at the breeder's one day and apparently fell in love with me on the spot. Lord knows why,' she added demurely. 'I was sold to them at a ridiculously discounted price, I might add, but the breeder told them I was a marvellous mouse catcher and this young couple had a chicken farm and wanted a cat to keep the mice from overrunning the place.'

'A mouse catcher,' Bertha interjected, with a hint of interest. 'Well, I can certainly relate to that.'

'I paid my dues, Bertha, I can tell you. If I wanted to eat, I had to hunt the horrible little rodents from dawn to dusk. But in return I was shown great affection and even allowed to share their couch and bed when I felt inclined. It was a difficult but nonetheless a very worthwhile experience.' She paused dramatically. 'But now, it's all gone so I decided to hit the road and seek adventure and a life of my own before I'm called to that great Vet in the Sky.'

Bertha had become totally transfixed by this sad turn of events that had blighted Millicent's life of fame and, although not in her usual nature, she felt a strange warmth towards this exotic creature, the like of which she had not felt since her younger days when she had fallen in love with a handsome feral ginger who had suffered the dreadful fate of being shot by an irate farmer who took offence at him killing a few of his geese.

'How about that drink?' Bertha said as she painfully dropped to the deck and led the way around to the back of the house.

Yes! exclaimed Millicent to herself, in triumph. Those boring drama classes at the Academy certainly come in handy. Now, let's check out the facilities and see if they come up to standard.

She followed the limping Bertha around to the back of the house and thirstily gulped some water from her red bowl by the back steps.

'Help yourself to some of that dried stuff too,' Bertha said as she indicated a matching bowl beside the water dish, which contained the remains of her last meal. 'It's vegetarian, I'm afraid. Rule of the house.'

'So, what's your story, Bertha?' Millicent said, as she delicately lapped the water and dipped her nose into the dried cat biscuits and began to chomp, resisting the urge to vomit.

'Not as glamorous as yours, I'm afraid,' she sighed, regretfully, as she sat and watched Millicent devour a couple of the hard brown morsels. 'Oh, I suppose I was a bit of a tear-away in my youth, I had some adventures …' she trailed off for a moment, remembering, 'but sadly those days are long gone. I'm basically a country girl now; had the same owners for years.'

Millicent flinched at the word 'owners' but let it pass.

'Pat and Jenny,' Bertha continued, 'lovely couple – they run the place. Luckily they adore cats in general and me in particular. But I'm sorry to say I can't pull my weight as I used to do. Those bloody mice and grasshoppers are getting faster, I swear. It's getting a bit out of hand.'

'Are there any other cats on the property?' Millicent asked innocently.

'No, not yet, but I'd say it's only a matter of time before they acquire another one. They'll probably keep me on as a pet though as they're pretty loyal and I keep them company more now than I used to – you know, jump on their laps when they're watching the tele and lie there dozing and purring a lot, although now it's more of a wheeze than a purr. I used to jump up on the kitchen bench when it was near feeding time, which used to make them laugh, but now it's a bit of an effort so I do a lot more rubbing myself on their legs to remind them to get my dinner out of the cupboard. Before, I could hunt and look after myself; there was always an easy meal to catch down near the chook pen, but as I said, the mice and lizards seem to be on pep pills these days.'

'Yes, the rubbing and purring are a bit demeaning but they always seem to get results,' Millicent remarked between chomps. 'They sometimes have to be reminded what the time is. I suppose the chase-the-furry-ball-on-the-end-of-a-string trick is a bit beyond you now, too?'

Bertha nodded sadly. 'Yes, those play times are long gone. It's even an effort to use the scratching pole now. Look at my nails, they're a mess. Jenny gives them the odd clip but it's not the same. They've even installed one of those litter trays in the bathroom in case I get caught short. Had a couple of – ahem, accidents – from time to time so they thought it best. Filthy things though, there's nothing better than being able to dig your own hole in the garden and fill it in when you've finished.'

'Couldn't agree more,' Millicent conceded. 'That litter never seems to cover the smell, does it?'

'Oh, they buy that odourless, clumping brand so it's not too bad,' replied Bertha. 'They originally bought that perfumed stuff but it played hell with my sinuses.'

Millicent swallowed the last of the biscuits and sat contentedly listening to Bertha while her mind went into overdrive. Well, so far, so good, she thought, but I'd better check out the facilities and options. The location is quite suitable; Bertha seems friendly and non-threatening, the owners could be amenable and there don't appear to be any other pets. If I play my cards right I should be able to infiltrate quite nicely. First, though, I'll explore the house and check for booby traps.

'Do they put you out of the house every night, Bertha?' she asked aloud.

'Oh no,' Bertha smiled. 'I have a pet flap in the back door. I come and go as I please. Gotta be quick when you're pushing through though, otherwise it slams you on the backside. Got a bad case of bursitis from that.'

A pet flap – another plus, thought Millicent. 'I don't suppose they have a computer out here? I mean the keyboard is great to sleep on.'

'Oh, yes,' replied Bertha. 'It's only an old one and it's on all the time. I sometimes have a nap on the tower – nice and warm, helps the arthritis. I also have a bit of a game with that fake mouse thing. Nothing too strenuous.'

And yet another plus, thought Millicent. She paused, twisted her head and licked the fur on her back and then said idly, 'How would you feel about me sort of hanging about for a while – visiting – just to catch my breath, so to speak. Just until I find a place of my own. Of course, I could turn feral and live out in the bush but the weather plays hell with my fur.'

Bertha joined in the fur grooming as she weighed up the pros and cons. 'Well, I don't see why not. It's certainly well worth the try. As I said, Pat and Jenny are confirmed cat people and they could be grateful for another set of claws to help out around the place. You'd have to do all that ingratiating bit, of course, but I get the feeling you'd be an expert in that field,' she said slyly. 'If you managed that and they accept you, we could maybe get around to doing a double act to keep them entertained – nothing too exerting, of course – and maybe sharing laps while they watch tele. So, what are you like at mouse hunting? I don't suppose you've had all that much experience, what with your breeding and being confined to cat shows.'

'I don't want to sound like I'm bragging,' Millicent mewed coyly, 'but it turned out I seemed to be a natural in that field. You said there was a chicken coop on the property. Why don't we take a little walk down there and I'll see what I can dig up.'

'Why not?' Bertha painfully stood on all four legs and disappeared into the back yard. 'Come on, I may be able to give you a few tips.'

Even in the fading darkness, Millicent, with her excellent night vision, took in the pleasant surroundings: a lovely green lawn divided by a stepping-stone path; a delightful terracotta bird bath; various shrubs; and some beautiful tall ghost gum trees with their wonderful silver bark trunks and brown patches curling off in small sheets, hanging down like curling brown paper. Excellent observation posts, Millicent noted. There were small, cement sculptures of naked women and exotic animals, green velvet lichen and ivy-covered stone walls with a tasteful arch that led through to an open field of vegetable beds and fruit trees.

Delightful, thought Millicent. This would suit my purposes admirably and I could be quite comfortable here.

Bertha led the way through the arch, then stopped and turned to Millicent. 'Okay,' she whispered, 'the chook pen is just around the corner there so keep low and creep up quietly. With a bit of luck the mice will be out eating the seed and vegetable peelings, the greedy little bastards. But the second they realise they're sprung they'll be back down their holes in a flash.'

Millicent slithered up to Bertha and, deferring to her expertise, she whispered, 'Okay, what's the plan?'

Bertha took a minute to peer through the shrub they were using for concealment to sum up their position and turned to Millicent. 'Right,' she said quietly, 'there are four targets in the middle of the pen. The gate is shut so we have to flush them out through the chicken wire and out into the open. We have to be careful they don't make a dive for their bunker – you see, over there in the corner of the pen under that perch? – and there's a tunnel out the other side of the netting. That's their usual MO.'

Millicent summed up their position and immed-iately her training came to the fore. 'Okay, we need to panic them. You act as the decoy and when they spot you they'll dash for their hole and I'll ambush them as they squeeze through the tunnel under the fence. I suggest you attack from the other end of the pen and flush them out. There're only four targets so together they should be a piece of cake. I'll hit them fast and furious and you can come around in support and help me mop up.'

Bertha nodded. 'Don't know how much help I'm going to be in my condition but I'll do my best.'

Millicent patted her on the shoulder in reassurance and Bertha slid away, creeping through the long grass and weeds to the far end of the pen. Millicent slithered in the opposite direction to her position, crouched and waited with her ears flattened, and every muscle tensed for action.

Suddenly, with a scream of hissing fury, Bertha threw herself at the netting and clung on, her paws clawing at the wire, her eyes flaring like a cat from hell, her fur standing out, her ragged bristling tail flailing. She was a frightening sight. Millicent could well understand what a fearsome opponent she must have been in her younger days.

The startled mice shrieked in terror, their little bodies involuntarily leaping in the air. The moment their tiny feet hit the ground they were off in a panic-driven rush for safety. As Millicent had predicted they dashed frantically for their hole, suddenly to be confronted by an unexpected opponent – Millicent the martial arts expert!

As the mice scurried under the fence Millicent attacked with the ferocity of a she-devil. '*Hajime!*' – 'Begin!' she screamed, and using her *yokoe ido* technique, she stepped to the side and quickly turned and used her *ushirogeri* – back kick – hitting two adversaries at the same time and sending them high into the air. Before they hit the ground shrieking, she had grabbed the third one in her powerful jaws, snapping its neck. The fourth mouse made the mistake of stopping suddenly in shock and before it had time to regain its momentum, Millicent used the *tobikomi* – jump forward movement, and snapped off its head with her razor-sharp teeth. She spat it on the ground and with lightning speed she engaged *uchi* – hit attack, on the third mouse and sent it flying and landing at the feet of Bertha who had made her way as quickly as she could to lend support. One large forepaw landed on the astonished mouse and it lay trapped under the part-Persian paw. It fainted in shock.

The fourth terrorist hit the ground running and Millicent flew through the air, scooped up the hapless mouse and tossed it high into the air. As it descended, tiny teeth bared in self-defence, she hit it with *sando zuki* – three vicious punches to the head and body sending it up into the air again. With perfect timing, Millicent used the *junzuki* – lunge or forward punch, hitting the mouse squarely in the head and sending it twirling through space to land at the feet of Bertha who quickly snapped its neck with her gums and sat there happily sucking its head.

The squawking chickens, which had become alarmed at the sudden and unexpected fury of the attack, gradually settled, clucked in appreciation of the skill of the kill, jumped back on their perches and promptly went back to sleep.

Surveying the corpses, Bertha mewed and began to purr. 'Say, we make a pretty good team, don't we?'

'It was certainly a bit of fun,' replied Millicent, beginning to lick the blood from her paws.

'Your moves were amazing,' said Bertha in obvious admiration. 'So graceful and fluid. Where did you learn those twists and turns? I've never seen anything quite like it.'

'It comes with the breeding,' replied Millicent, demurely. 'Now, let's drag these corpses up onto the back deck for a bit of a trophy display, eh? That should impress the staff ... I mean, Pat and Jenny.'

'It certainly will,' purred Bertha. 'This is our first cull for months.'

By the time the golden sun had begun to peek over the surrounding hills and trees, the morning light bore witness to a pile of ten dead mice arranged on the deck outside the back door for inspection. A partnership had been formed and the C team had done its work well.

Exhausted from their night's work, the new comrades rested; Bertha lay sprawled out with her nose pointing directly at the pile of trophies while Millicent slept, curled up further away on the other side of the back door. Suddenly the door opened and Millicent's eyes sprang wide whilst, to all intents and purposes, still remaining ostensibly asleep.

'Ahhh!' she heard a startled female gasp. 'Jenny, get out here and take a look at this! You won't believe it!'

'What is it?' replied another female voice.

'Look! Bertha's left us a little present!' the first woman's voice called, followed by a low chuckle.

Millicent rose to her feet, arranged herself in her customary 'model' pose, head high, feet together and tail neatly curled around her paws, and sat waiting. The first woman, obviously Pat, she assumed, was a rather stocky lady with beefy shoulders and arms, short, black hair which stuck out in spikes, a bit like one of those floating mines Millicent had seen in old World War II navy films on the tele. She was in her mid to late thirties in human terms, Millicent estimated, with a wide, beaming, friendly face at the moment as she studied the mass of mutilated mice. She was garbed in rather baggy workpants that had seen better days, and a check-patterned, bogan work shirt with the long sleeves rolled up above her elbows to display rather fetching Polynesian tattoos. She wore a subtle silver ring in her left ear but no jewellery on her hands. Her feet were clad in heavy leather work boots.

The other woman, Jenny, arrived at the door carrying a pack of dried cat food. Millicent naturally assumed this was for Bertha's breakfast and not her own because she was far too young to eat pensioner food. Jenny gave a squeal of delight at the sight of the night's hunting expedition, scooped Bertha up and cuddled her.

'What a good girl you are!' Then turning to Pat she said, 'That's a first for a while. Maybe she's feeling better.'

Jenny was almost the opposite of Pat with long blonde-streaked hair framing a pretty, heart-shaped face. She was much slimmer than her partner with long slender legs that showed through the opening of the pale blue floral dressing gown she was wearing. Her voice was gentler than Pat's and Millicent decided she would be a pushover.

Both women continued to make a fuss of Bertha who purred and luxuriated in their attention while the overlooked Millicent sat watching.

Okay, enough is enough, Millicent decided, time for my performance. She got to her feet, mewed softly and limped pitifully towards the two women.

Catching sight of her, Jenny squeaked again. 'What's this? Pat, look at this. Where did you come from?' she gushed in pleasure. 'What an exotic-looking pussy!'

Pat picked Millicent up and laid her back in the crook of her elbow, a position Millicent wasn't entirely happy in but was prepared to accept under the circumstances.

'Well,' said Pat, studying Millicent carefully, 'she must be new to the area. A fine-looking Oriental Shorthair, I'd say. They're not all that common. I've seen pictures of the breed in some of our cat magazines. They're sort of a Siamese cross. I wonder who she belongs to. Surely she's not from next door, they're dog people.'

Oops, thought Millicent, better keep an eye out for that.

'And I noticed she was limping a bit too,' continued Pat, closely examining Millicent. 'She seems to have a bit of a scratch on her hind leg, or it could be a bite. I wonder if Bertha had a bit of help from this little moggie on last night's safari.'

Moggie? Millicent was affronted. Moggie! *Moi*?

'We'll have to ask around and see who she belongs to,' said Pat. 'Maybe the vet would know if she's been reported missing. It says on her name tag her name is Millicent.'

'Millicent? Milly, that's a cute name for her,' said Jenny.

Milly? Millicent inwardly fumed. And *cute?* Oh God, what a girl has to put up with for the sake of her profession.

'In the meantime,' said Pat, 'let's get them both inside and check them over for any more damage.'

'Her paws look a little frayed, don't you think?' Jenny observed, gently spreading Millicent's paws. 'She looks like she's been on a big walk. Maybe she's a stray.'

'I'd say Millicent might have had a bit of a hand in the mouse hunt last night,' said Pat.

'See,' said Jenny as she held the two cats' heads close together, 'I told you we should get another cat as a friend for Bertha. They seem to get on okay with each other.'

'Well, let's not jump the gun, Jen. Let's wait to see if anyone claims her before we go making any plans for her, eh?'

'Okay, love, but she is very pretty. If she does turn out to be a stray, can we keep her?'

'We'll see,' smiled Pat indulgently.

Ah, sighed Millicent as she was carried inside the house. A little bit of obsequiousness always brings results.

Chapter 3

That afternoon, as Millicent was taking advantage of the cooler air on the back verandah and Bertha was snoozing on the window sill above, establishing her dominance in the household, Pat clumped up the stairs, pulled off her boots and slipped into her house thongs. She had been watering, trimming, weeding and mulching the vegetable crop in the back paddock all morning while Jenny had been baking and cleaning. The smell of freshly baked cake wafted in the air. Millicent stirred herself, stretched seductively, and gave Pat a friendly mew and purr as Pat passed through into the house.

She heard a quiet exchange of conversation between the two women but, even with her excellent sense of hearing, she couldn't quite make out what was being said. She was soon to find out.

After a few minutes, Pat appeared carrying a hideous pink plastic pet pack and placed it on the deck. She then gently lifted Millicent with one hand while opening the pet pack door grille with the other.

Uh-oh. Millicent cringed and started to struggle. What the hell was going on? Pat didn't think she was going to incarcerate her in *that* thing, did she? She never travelled in a *pet pack!*

But in spite of her loud protests, Pat expertly restrained her flailing legs and arms, and ignoring her struggles and loud demands to be released, gently but firmly deposited her in the pet pack and slid the locking bar in place.

Have I been over confident? Millicent asked herself, Too sure of myself? Did I mistake the signs? Are they going to take me somewhere and dump me by the side of the road? Or into a dam or a river, weighed down with rocks?

Her mind spun as she re-examined her actions and Pat and Jenny's response to her arrival.

No, can't be, I followed all the rules. They fell for it, I'm sure.

Pat tried to soothe her. 'Now, calm down, little girl, don't be frightened. We're just going to take you into town to visit the vet. We want to have that back paw checked out and see if you've been micro chipped, which would tell us who you belong to and where you come from.'

'I belong to me!' Millicent screamed, but to Pat it came out as an angry shriek. 'And I don't need a vet! I simply pulled a nail when I performed that reverse *ashi barai* – foot sweep – on that stupid mouse when that *gedan barai* – lower block – didn't quite come off. So I was too close to the chicken wire – we all make mistakes! I'll just lick it and apply some of that aloe vera you've got growing in the front garden. I don't need a vet!'

'Well, there doesn't seem to be anything wrong with your vocal chords, little one,' Pat laughed. 'C'mon Jen,' she called out. 'Millicent's getting a little restive.'

Jenny came through the back door dressed in a long flowing silk caftan in bright pink and orange, and from her blonde head, a lime green scarf trailed down almost to the ground.

My God, thought Millicent, I hope we're travelling in the truck and not an open sports car, otherwise Jenny's liable to be doing an Isadora Duncan.

As luck would have it, Pat placed the pet pack in the back of the old utility that Millicent had noted when she had first arrived, and secured a hemp rope to keep the pack from falling off. The two women got in the front cabin, the motor roared into life and they took off with wheels spinning madly on the gravel driveway, sending up tiny bits of rock in their wake.

'Whoa! Pat's obviously into drag racing,' Millicent gasped, clinging onto the bars of the cage.

The ute hit the bitumen and the ride became smoother. Millicent calmed down and settled on the old, red, crushed-velvet cloth lying folded on the floor of the pack. Hmmm, she purred, red velvet. Well, that's a little more like it, at least. And she began to plan her strategy while taking in the passing scenery as they made their way out onto the bitumen highway and turned toward the town.

The town, or more correctly, the village, was only small compared to the cities she had been assigned to on other cases. They headed down Cullen Street, the main and one of the few roads of the town, it seemed, and past the yellow and blue Regional Gallery and Community Centre. A small park was set on the corner of Sibley Street with a few rather striking cream-coloured stone sculptures of giant faces.

Looking out through the bars of the pet pack Millicent was surprised to see the colourful psychedelic murals that covered many of the store fronts with names like Happy High Herbs, Rainbow Love, Rainbow Piercing and Custom Tattoos, Stoned Fish Cafe and The Hemp Embassy.

Well, it certainly looks like I've arrived in Hippy Heaven, she thought. Maybe I should get an ear pierced or maybe my tail? I don't want to stand out.

The veterinary surgery was close to the centre of Nimbin and Pat had difficulty finding a parking space in the town's car park. She had to park blocks away from the surgery and carry the offensive pink pet pack with the mortally embarrassed Millicent ensconced inside feeling like a precocious, spoiled, Toorak debutante.

That's it! she suddenly exclaimed to herself in a flash of inspiration. I'll put on my dignified, precious, pampered show cat performance!

After all, she'd performed this specialty many times in the face of uncertainty and indecision.

I'll be so aloof the vet will be intimidated into treating me with the respect and consideration a champion show cat deserves. I'll retain a lofty disposition and take my time observing and sourcing out information.

They entered the reception area and Millicent was relieved to notice the place was spotlessly clean and almost welcoming with a fetching mural of green frogs painted near the entrance. Only two other patients, a motley pair of hounds of the mongrel variety, and their young bearded owner, also of inferior breed by the look of him, sat waiting for their treatment. I hope the young man is in for a bath and clip, she observed, noting the grubby, lank, second-hand clothes and dreadlocks.

The stupid canines set to barking and straining at their leashes to get at her of course, but she simply hissed, spat and scratched at their noses when they got too close and arched her stiff bristled back, and the stupid dogs soon retreated with a yelp to silently sit and watch her, wondering what strange sort of parents had produced such a weird-looking animal, the like of which they had never seen before.

Pat lifted the pack onto the counter out of harm's way and Millicent suddenly noticed sitting at the end the receptionist's counter with a regal look of disdain, the most beautiful male Burmese cat she had ever seen. He was not restrained in any way and elegantly glided along the counter to inspect this new arrival.

The receptionist was absent from her desk, obviously assisting the vet with a troublesome patient, judging from the bleats coming from the inside of the surgery, and Pat and Jenny had taken seats while they waited to be attended.

'Well,' purred the Burmese, 'what have we here?' He sniffed the cage and examined the exotic 'prisoner' now suddenly coyly submissive to this gorgeous and no doubt esteemed representative of Burmese royalty. 'I do believe you're an Oriental Shorthair. I declare I haven't seen another one of your variety around here. And where do you hail from, my pretty?'

Millicent's heart began to race at the sight of this magnificent shiny brown creature with piercing golden eyes and the lithe body of a panther. 'Well,' she gulped, while thinking to herself, so much for the precious, pampered, show cat act. This luscious life form makes me feel as vulnerable as a day-old kitten. 'I'm holidaying at the Dunroamin estate on the outskirts of town,' she replied, as haughtily as she could manage.

'Dunroamin,' he said, his yellow eyes widening in surprise. 'I know it well. I thought the matronly Bertha was the only cat in residence. When did you arrive?' he purred quietly as he seductively rubbed himself against the side of the pink pet pack, sending involuntary shivers up Millicent's spine.

'Actually, only last night,' replied Millicent, trying desperately to compose herself. 'Bertha and I are old friends from way back – not related of course,' she improvised. 'She was a friend of my mother's. She's getting on a bit and I heard she was having a bit of trouble hunting and keeping the mouse population under control so naturally I offered to help.'

'Ah, a kind heart, a hunter *and* an exquisite beauty,' he purred. 'I've always had a soft spot for Oriental Shorthairs and you're obviously a perfect specimen – a positive show winner,' he said appraisingly. 'And what is your name, my sleek-haired friend?'

'Millicent,' she mumbled, her blush thankfully not showing beneath her fur.

'Millicent,' he repeated thoughtfully, committing it to memory. 'And why are you visiting my vet, Dr Fellini? You look in absolute peak condition, if I may say so.' His tone was soft and seductive.

'Oh, it's just a check-up. I had a slight accident last night when I was hunting – just a slight scratch on my back paw – it's nothing. But my staff are so caring and protective, they advised an appointment with your Dr Fellini, just to be on the safe side.'

'Very wise, I'm sure. We purebreds can't be too careful.' He stared at her from beneath his lustrous brows and fine dark whiskers. 'And what is your background, Millicent?'

'Oh, just the usual, you know – pampered pet, decorative – showbiz,' she added as she arched her back and stretched languidly.

'And where was this?'

'Down south, 'she replied vaguely.

The door to the surgery opened and Dr Fellini escorted his patient and its owner out. Millicent was surprised to see the patient was a small white goat. The kid was limping, which matched the owner's gait; an elderly gentleman with a short, grey beard and long grey straggly hair that reached to his thin, bony shoulders. 'There's a perfect example of the owners growing to look like their pet,' she said light heartedly, attempting to bring a little levity into the awkward moment.

'Thank you, Mr Boer,' said the vet. 'Gillie's coming along fine; just keep an eye on that leg and on her diet. And no more aluminium cans, eh?'

The elderly gentleman mumbled his thanks, paid the receptionist who had returned to her desk and led the bleating goat out the front door. The stupid dogs scrambled to their feet and barked insanely, of course, but the young man restrained them.

'Pat and Jenny, you might as well come in next,' said the vet. 'I'm just waiting for the pharmacist to send over some injections for these,' he said indicating the two dogs now scratching furiously as they sat at their owner's feet.

Pat and Jenny stood and headed for Millicent on the counter. 'Hello, King,' Jenny said as she stroked the Burmese who purred in response while Pat lifted the pink pet pack from the counter. 'What a beautiful boy you are.'

King – what a perfect name for such a regal-looking cat, Millicent thought, as Dr Fellini opened the door and ushered them into the surgery. King swiftly leapt from the counter and through the door before it could close. Silently and sure-footedly, he immediately jumped onto a filing cabinet near the treatment table to watch proceedings.

'And what can I do for you three ladies?' asked Dr Fellini, who had a slight accent.

Dr Fellini appeared to be a man in his late thirties, slim, olive complexioned, with dark, slightly waved hair, trimmed to just below his ears. His eyes were intense and almost black. His accent suggested European migration. Millicent's first impression was that he was most likely, and understandably, a very successful womaniser.

'Well,' said Jenny, 'Millicent here arrived at the farm last night out of the blue and when we discovered her this morning she and Bertha had left us a lovely present in the form of a pile of dead mice. We don't know where she came from but she is very beautiful and we thought you may be able to check and see if she's been micro chipped. We'd love to keep her, of course, as she and Bertha seem to get on so well together and they're such good company for each other. But naturally, if we can find her owners, we'll contact them and let them know she's safe and well.'

'And of course,' added Pat, 'if we can find them, we'll return her to her owners. But she also seems to have a cut or a scratch on her left hind paw and we thought it may need treatment.'

'I see,' said Dr Fellini. 'Ok, let's first check for a chip and see what we can find out.'

He opened the lid of the pet pack and lifted Millicent onto the examination table. Millicent was quite comfortable being examined by such an attractive vet and didn't attempt to jump off the table. She merely sat quite still in her perfectly posed, Gold Medal position and looked around the surgery. King watched appreciatively from the filing cabinet, taking in her fine lines.

Dr Fellini took a scanner from a shelf as he said, 'She's an excellent example of an Oriental Shorthair – quite expensive, I'd say. I should imagine her owners would be quite worried about her disappearance.'

'Yes, that's what I told Jen,' said Pat.

Dr Fellini ran the instrument over the back of Millicent's neck.

'Ah, yes, here it is.' He looked at the number displayed on the back of the scanner and moved to a computer, brought up the program he was looking for and entered the number.

'Ah, here we are,' he said, reading from the monitor. 'Yes, it says here her name is Millicent and …' There was a long pause before he continued, 'Well, I don't know, ladies; it says here the owner is a Mr A Scratchpole and the address given is … 24 Orchid Way, Canberra! Well, Millicent,' he said as he stroked her head, 'you are a long way from home, aren't you?'

Too far away to send me back, that's for sure, smirked Millicent.

'I'd say she's been moved up here to a strange state and gone wandering before the owners could change the information on the chip,' said Fellini. 'They usually have an excellent sense of direction, but I don't think she'd have the ability to get back to Canberra or find her way back to her new home. She's obviously travelled some distance from the look of her paws. I'll put some medication on that scratch and clean it up but they usually self-heal very well.'

'Do you think it's alright to keep her at the farm?' asked Jenny.

'I don't see why not,' replied the vet. 'You could put up a few posters around the place advertising where she is if you want to, and I'll keep an ear out for anyone who may come looking for her.'

'Right,' said Pat, 'we'll do that.'

King sat on the filing cabinet taking it all in. His face showed little, of course, but his mind was working very meticulously.

Dr Fellini gave Millicent a thorough check over, running his sensitive hands over her body and down over her tail. 'Kidneys and other vital organs seem in excellent condition,' he said, and then gently lifted her rear off the table by the tail and stuck a thermometer up her bum.

Oops, Millicent jumped, startled. I wasn't quite expecting that, Doc, a bit more warning next time, thank you. She glanced across the room at King who was sitting watching very attentively. Oh, how embarrassing, thought Millicent, and we've only just met.

'Temperature's fine,' said the vet, 'so all in all, a very healthy specimen.'

Dr Fellini bathed Millicent's wound and applied an antiseptic cream which Millicent immediately began to lick off as soon as she was returned to the dreaded pet pack. Pat and Jenny paid the bill and left. King returned to his position on the reception counter and Dr Fellini bent and whispered in his ear, 'I think we should keep an eye on that one, King, I didn't say anything but I think she may be wearing a wire embedded under her collar. She could be a spy.'

King responded with an inscrutable look and began to lick his paws.

As they made their way back to the ute, Jenny said she wanted to do a bit of shopping and asked Pat if they could have a cup of coffee before they returned home. Pat agreed and said she and Millicent would sit at an outside table at the Rainbow Coffee Shop and wait for her.

This was an excellent opportunity for Millicent to observe the immediate area and she peered through the bars of the pet pack soaking up the sights, smells and sounds of the town. From her limited view, she spied several shops that could be of interest: a hippy gift shop psychedelically painted on the outside with murals of the bush and colourful birds; a couple of food shops, also colourfully painted in bright colours, with tables outside on the footpath holding bottles and jars of local produce; a chemist, rather utilitarian; and clothes shops with racks of weird garments hanging outside offering everything from bright kaftans with sequins and beads, hand-woven capes and drab dresses, to funny-looking knitted hats of all shapes and sizes, and ugly second-hand shoes.

Well, there goes the chance of a Gucci collar, she thought.

Awnings and tall dense-leafed trees shaded the footpaths and pedestrians lingered and chatted in the streets. Obviously there were quite a few tourists visiting and they stood out a mile from the locals with their alternative appearance and lifestyles. Millicent noticed a couple of young locals stopping and chatting to passing pedestrians in a conspiratorial way. Sometimes she saw what was obviously a secretive exchange of money for small packets of drugs, but no one seemed to be taking much notice. Her sensitive sense of smell picked up the distinct odour of incense and cannabis in the air sometimes and a few of the locals appeared obviously stoned, but serene. On the whole, from her limited view from beside the coffee table, the town appeared to have a very quiet and peaceful ambiance – maybe too quiet and peaceful, she pondered. She detected an air of secrecy that could not be ignored.

Chapter 4

And so it came about that Millicent took up residence in the small permaculture farm holding known as Dunroamin. Over the coming weeks, Pat checked with the vet and even put up signs around the village but to no avail. No one came forward to claim the funny-looking fabulous feline.

To cement her position in the household, Millicent made sure that she and Bertha became close friends and conducted nightly forays on the mice population with great results to the joy and great satisfaction of Pat and Jenny. Although Millicent gradually became part of the family as far as Pat, Jenny and the bumbling Bertha were concerned, she was forced to keep her natural aloofness down to a minimum to achieve this, and her eye steadfastly on her mission. She forced herself to be playful and 'cute' even though it felt a trifle demeaning.

She now felt secure and had the run of the place and quickly discovered the home office with its old solid maple desk, grey metal filing cabinet, blue and green floral armchair, and solid maple timber bookshelves cluttered with a collection of books on organic farming – obviously Pat's interest; Di Morrissey and other romantic novels, even a couple of Barbara Cartlands – obviously Jenny's favourites; travel books, and a whole shelf of Eastern and alternative philosophy editions.

In front of the desk was a black leather swivel chair with a purple-fringed throw-over, and sitting on top of the desk was … the computer! It was a rather outdated model compared to the ones Millicent had been used to but it was connected to broadband and it worked as well as could be expected. Best of all it was always turned on and booted up, ready to go.

During the night when the household was asleep, Millicent emailed the Agency to inform Tom of her safe arrival and her current location and brought him up to date on what had been happening. The emails had been confirmed and Millicent knew exactly where to find them. All communication was in code, of course, and she knew neither Pat nor Jenny would recognise the sender's address and immediately delete it. Millicent simply went into the 'deleted items' file, found her messages, and replied.

She quickly established the habit of taking turns of curling up on Jenny or Pat's lap in the evenings while they watched television. The chosen lap had a lot to do with which lap Bertha had chosen to ensconce herself on and Millicent ensured that Bertha always had the first choice, so as not to usurp Bertha's position and run the risk of putting her offside. Although Millicent appeared to be snoozing, her hearing was always on full alert to pick up any idle gossip that may be of use to her. That's how she gained the intelligence on the adjacent farm, 'Binthere-Dunthat'. Apparently it was owned by a mysterious recluse by the name of Reg, and his two roughneck sons, Mick and Jacko.

Millicent heard Pat telling Jenny she was a bit suspicious of the number of visitors that frequented the farm for short visits. Binthere-Dunthat was ostensibly a small-holding farm that grew and supplied tomatoes to cafés and small food stores in town but the number of visitors didn't seem to warrant that limited trade. Pat subtly inferred that perhaps tomatoes weren't their only crop and she'd seen the two roughneck sons driving around in an expensive new SUV. As far as she was aware the boys didn't appear to have any other regular work and it would take a lot of tomatoes to pay for an expensive car like that. She snidely suggested that they were maybe into 'another sort of crop' like many other plantations around the area.

Seeing it was only a small acreage, the authorities hadn't seemed to have got around to inspecting the property for a long time and their limited staff was kept very busy searching for the larger dealers who were into serious amounts of amphetamines and the like.

'Still, drugs are drugs,' Pat remonstrated angrily, and the sordid history of her parents and other heavy users she had literally seen come and go had made her fiercely anti-drugs and suspicious of any such abuses of the law.

It seemed that both Pat and Jenny had been born into families of drug, alcohol and physical abuse and had both been victims of the incalculable damage it caused. In fact, that had been the main factor that had brought them together many years prior. They had both been from poor city neighbourhoods and clung together for love and support as there was certainly none available within their families and circle of acquaintances. They had finally worked very hard at any job they could find and saved enough money to escape to the country.

Nimbin was a strange place to choose, Millicent thought, with its well-established history of drug trading, but it also had a strong reputation of community support, and the country around was certainly beautiful, fertile and far removed from the squalor of city life. At that time land was relatively affordable and the soil rich for organic growing. Pat and Jenny, like many of the other inhabitants, were determined to escape the pressures and turmoils in which society was enslaving them and achieve a peaceful existence together on the land and become self-supporting.

They had studied and mastered permaculture farming and believed this would make them self-sufficient, bringing them closer to the true wealth of the earth rather than the false wealth of advertising, commercialism, processed food and the inherent corporate greed that led people inexorably into stress and enforced labour in order to conform. Yes, they had 'opted out' of what was considered modern society and, sensibly, only retained that which was helpful to them to sustain their existence and relative comfort, and they were very happy.

Perhaps their chosen lifestyle was what brought about the kindness, tolerance, peace and tranquillity that imbued their home. Millicent recognised and admired the simple spirituality and respect for the life force that pervaded her new safe house. But she also knew, in her own way, she was fighting for the same thing. There were the peace lovers and there were the warriors to protect the simple, unsophisticated, gentle souls. And she was one of the warriors.

Chapter 5

The night was dark with the moon hidden behind banks of heavy cloud that only occasionally allowed it to peek through and cast its silver light over the countryside. Millicent had decided to investigate the adjacent property and try to discover the secrets that lay hidden in the shadows of the buildings and shrubbery that concealed it from prying eyes.

Bertha had been sleeping soundly on the back verandah so did not notice her new-found friend slip down the stairs and into the darkness. Silently and with the stealth of felinity, in which she was a trained expert, Millicent cautiously made her way across the lawn to the borderline and through the undergrowth toward the neighbouring property. She absorbed the sights, sounds, smells and textures as she advanced, ever watchful of danger and particularly tuned to the presence of the ferocious dogs that reportedly roamed and guarded the area.

Dogs held little fear for Millicent as she was also well trained in the art of self-defence in response to canine attack. Many had been the time when she was confronted with the brutal creatures and her intelli-gence, dexterity and enormous turn of speed had often saved her from a grisly, mutilated death. However, avoidance of conflict, with the accompanying sounds of battle and the inevitable furious barking, was imperative if her advance into enemy territory and local intelligence-gathering was to be successful.

At first she investigated the fields of tomato vines and other vegetable plots and with her excellent training and sense of smell soon confirmed Pat's suspicions. There was indeed a sizeable crop of cannabis cunningly concealed, interspersed with the tomatoes and other plants.

As she explored, she suddenly became instinctively uncomfortable and suspicious of movement from somewhere behind her and quickly froze in her tracks. She crouched behind a stand of celery, her eyes and ears searching out the source of the movement. Although she strained, every nerve sensitive to a stalker, her senses only detected silence and stillness. She waited for some time to confirm her suspicions but when nothing eventuated, she decided she was mistaken or being overly cautious. It must have been another mouse or maybe a lizard hunting for insects, she decided, and with no further evidence of a pursuer continued on her way.

It didn't appear to be a large commercial-sized crop of cannabis but it would certainly be enough for personal use with enough left over to provide a comfortable income. She quickly estimated the amount and value and filed it away in her memory bank for her Agency report. She then turned her attention to the sheds and outhouses, examining any possible nook or cranny that may conceal some hidden clue to any other form of drug production, but most provided only evidence of an ordinary farm with innocent constructions, appliances and tools.

But there was still the unmistakable smell of cannabis in the air. Mice were prevalent everywhere but she ignored them, deciding she would snack later, when she had finished her investigation. My God, she thought, the little rodents are in plague proportions in this neck of the woods. I could survive for years around here.

She slipped through a hole in a wall where a board had come loose and discovered to her surprise a hidden cellar containing shelves stacked with small plastic bags containing a stash of dried dope. Ah, this was more like it. She noted poison pellets scattered around to dissuade the mice but it was obvious the devious little devils had ignored the danger and attacked several of the bags as was evidenced by the little holes chewed in some of them, and piles of mouse droppings.

Suddenly she heard the unmistakable sound of scratching and sniffing, louder than any mouse could make, and she crouched low and still to ascertain the direction from which it was coming. The sound stopped and she crept forward again finding the opening of a pipe drain which she entered. The sound started again but there was no sign of the perpetrator within the drain and she continued up the pipe warily. The sound stopped again as she came to the end of the pipe and peeked out. There was a sudden scurrying sound and she was confronted with a sight that chilled her soul – a monstrous rodent!

My God, she thought, this mouse has certainly been hitting the steroids! The monster's eyes glowed red and its sharp teeth were bared in anger. She automatically retaliated by squatting, spitting, hissing and displaying her own fangs in defence.

'Don't even think of it, pussy,' hissed the rat. 'I could have you for supper! One move and I'll tear ya throat out.'

This necessitated serious contemplation and Millicent carefully began to back down the pipe to make her escape as there was no room to turn. The rat edged its way to the opening of the pipe and glared down at her. She hissed and spat again which gave the rat cause to pause as Millicent continued to back out of her trapped position.

'You're wasting your time, sweetie,' the rat squeaked, 'my friend Jake is waiting for you at the other end.' It chuckled evilly.

Millicent froze, her mind whirling, trying to work out a way of escape from her trapped position. Well, she'd been in tight places before and managed to extricate herself. Although discretion was the better part of valour, backing out of the pipe was not an option and a frontal confrontation seemed inevitable. She would have to charge forward and meet the monster head on. She knew he would go for her throat, which was partly protected by her steel impregnated collar, but it was going to be a fierce battle all the same. Speed and guile was the order of the day. She hunched her shoulder and thigh muscles, bared her teeth and prepared to launch herself at the foe.

Suddenly there were two distinct, separate, short, sharp, spitting sounds and the rat flinched, twitched violently, opened its jaws in a hideous grimace, its eyes still flaring red, before they suddenly clamped shut, its body twitched and it dropped lifeless to the ground. Millicent crouched, astonished at this unexpected development. Slowly the monstrous creature seemed to be sliding back away from the pipe opening as if being dragged backwards. King's beautiful and welcome face appeared at the mouth of the drainpipe. His sparkling golden eyes smiled down at her.

'Got yourself into a bit of a dicey situation there, Milly. You city girls should take a little more care when you're out exploring the neighbourhood.'

'*Millicent*,' she retorted archly, appalled at appear-ing incompetent in the face of her strong saviour, but secretly relieved that King had arrived when he had.

'I had the situation well under control, thank you very much,' she said as she crawled out of the pipe.

King smiled indulgently and stepped back to allow her to extricate herself from the drain. Millicent emerged and immediately examined the rat to ascertain the damage King had inflicted. Strangely she could see no evidence of mauling present on the corpse. King bent over the body and with his sharp teeth extracted a small dart from the beast's hindquarters.

'What's that?' asked Millicent, in a quandary.

'Oh, nothing,' replied King evasively as he spat the dart onto the ground. 'It's just a dart.'

'A dart?' queried Millicent. 'What sort of dart?''

'Poison tipped,' King replied, nonchalantly.

'What?' Millicent retorted in astonishment. 'But how did it get there?'

'Blowpipe,' King answered shortly, indicating the dead rat at his feet.

'But how on earth did you manage to do that?' Millicent asked astounded.

King stood on his hind legs and fiddled at an area on his upper stomach. He caught a claw in the eye of a zip and pulled it open to reveal a pouch!

'What are you, some sort of kangaroo cross?' Millicent asked amazed.

King chuckled. 'Not really.'

'But how …?' Millicent was lost for words and the question went unasked.

'Well,' answered King, 'I've had a bit of plastic surgery done. An experiment, actually. But it's come in pretty handy to carry things around.'

'Vivisection?' exclaimed Millicent, horrified.

'Well, hardly,' chortled King. 'A bit of a nip and tuck improvement, that's all.' He put his paw into the pouch and pulled out a short blowpipe. 'It's based on one of the original Burmese tribe's weapons – very handy really.'

'But your paw, it's so much more flexible than usual. You can use your claws independently! It's almost like a human hand!'

'Yeah, another handy extra,' he smiled.

'I don't understand,' said Millicent, in confusion.

'Now, don't get your whiskers in a wrangle,' he said in an attempt to pacify her. 'I'm just a prototype. No big deal.' He returned the blowpipe to his pouch and zipped it up.

'What else do you carry in that … pouch thing?' she asked.

'Oh, just bits and pieces,' he replied airily.

'Were you following me out there in the fields?' Millicent asked, suspiciously.

King gave that maddening smile again but did not reply.

'But why didn't you make yourself known to me?' she asked.

'I was just curious to see what you were up to,' he replied.

'Well, as they say,' she retorted in annoyance, 'curiosity killed the cat.'

He smiled sagely and indicated the body of the rat. 'As they say. But this time it killed the rat.'

But before she could continue berating him, a loud barking from quite nearby interrupted her. 'We'd better get out of here,' King urged her. 'The mongrels are on the loose and have picked up our scent and I've run out of darts.' He began to edge her toward the door but she stopped.

'Why are you here tonight, anyway? You're a long way from home.'

'I was just out on my nightly prowl,' he answered as he urged her forward, 'and found myself in your neck of the woods. I spotted you sniffing around and thought I'd better keep an eye on you – just for safety's sake. Just as well I did, don't you think?'

She had no answer to that and the two of them shot through the door and headed back to Dunroamin followed by the raucous baying of hounds at their heels. Of course they were much too fast for the dogs and soon outdistanced them. They paused when they reached the safety of the stairs that led to the back deck.

'Well,' said Millicent, a little exhilarated, 'that was a bit of an adventure.'

He smiled at her mischievously. 'I don't suppose a snack or a nightcap would be appropriate?' he suggested hopefully.

'I think not,' replied Millicent coolly, although other basic instincts were definitely coming into play. 'I have a headache and I'm very tired and we wouldn't want to wake Bertha or Pat and Jenny, would we?'

Besides, she thought, there was much to think about and she really should hit the computer and get a message to Tom.

King looked a bit crestfallen but accepted the refusal with equanimity. 'Well,' he purred, 'perhaps I'll see you around?'

Millicent nodded almost reluctantly and turned to walk up the stairs. She stopped on the top step and turned to him. 'King ... thank you so much for looking after me tonight. You're quite the gentleman, aren't you, rescuing the maiden in distress?'

'My pleasure – glad to be of assistance,' he replied gallantly and he turned and walked away.

Millicent watched his sensual walk as he disappeared around the corner of the farmhouse.

There's more to that gorgeous cat than meets the eye, she mused, thoughtfully.

'And did we have a good night?' came Bertha's sleepy but amused voice from her corner of the deck.

Millicent shrugged. 'So-so,' she replied as she pushed her way through the pet flap and into the house.

Chapter 6

Over the following weeks Millicent's position within the household became even stronger by her determined efforts to ingratiate herself into Pat and Jenny's affections. They had attempted to fit her with a harness and lead which she flatly rejected and demonstrated that she was perfectly capable of, and indeed, preferred riding in the back of the ute or unhindered in the cabin when they went out. Pat usually wore a backpack and Millicent was quite content to lie curled on the top of the pack with her head on Pat's shoulder as she and Jenny walked, shopped or browsed. They thought it amusing and enjoyed the reactions of passers-by at this endearing habit. It also gave Millicent the opportunity to study the terrain and the characters of the town more closely.

From her elevated position she absorbed the goings-on of the town and was able to spy out possible matters of interest. For example, she could recognise many of the old locals who had obviously lived in the area for years, and who, most probably, were some of the original European inhabitants who had moved to the area in the early seventies when they were young and vibrant; peace-loving hippies attracted by the Age of Aquarius Festival and the alternative lifestyle. Now, of course, many of those who survived and remained had grown old and some looked rather sad, realising too late perhaps that many of the benefits of modern life had passed them by and they were left disillusioned. Or was that just another symptom of old age?

But many were still young and eager to embrace the social freedoms the community encouraged and were obviously thriving; or maybe they were all stoned? There was no doubt the surrounding countryside was glorious but Millicent knew the natural beauty was sometimes infected by noxious weeds; pockets of greedy opportunists whose clandestine behaviour brought destruction and disrupted the peace and tranquillity. Ah, she mused philosophically, such has always been the way of humanity, and that is the reason I am here, she reminded herself, to protect the innocent and an idyllic way of life.

Millicent had learned from her research prior to her deployment that Nimbin was 785 kilometres north of Sydney in the Northern Rivers district, with a relatively small local permanent community of only a few hundred people. It was now surrounded by beautiful world heritage national parks and enjoyed a sub-tropical, warm temperate climate, which encouraged rainforests to spring from the rhyolite and rich basalt soil. It held a special place in Bundjalung Aboriginal culture reaching back to the Dreamtime and is the believed resting place of the Rainbow Serpent and protector, Warrajum. It was considered a place of healing and initiation.

The word 'Nimbin' derived from the legend of the Nimbinjee people, and the ancient sleeping warrior of the Nightcap Range, like the famous Nimbin Rocks, is believed to lie ever watchful over the village and surrounds. Although European settlers penetrated the valley in the mid nineteenth century in search of the timber so abundant in the area, the successful but somewhat destructive industry slowly declined during the early twentieth century and the cleared land was turned into a thriving dairy and banana-growing district.

But the Aquarius Festival in 1973, a counter-culture expo and arts festival organised by the Australian Union of Students, and the subsequent festival of 2003, revitalised the area with the influx of new settlers seeking to create an alternative lifestyle to escape the hectic and restrictive commercialism and stress of the modern cities. Only a short distance from the village were to be found unrivalled natural beauties of the dramatic, extinct volcanic landscapes, lush subtropical rainforests, musical waterfalls, reflective rock pools and bewitching native flora and fauna to captivate the senses. Millicent was delighted with this particular posting.

'Come on, Millicent, we're going off for a nice picnic,' Pat said one day as she scooped the dozing Millicent up from the couch.
'What?' Millicent yelled with a start as she was promptly placed in her now accustomed position on the blue backpack.
'It's a pity poor old Bertha can't come with us,' sighed Jenny.
'I know, love,' said Pat, 'but she really isn't up to it anymore. She may as well stay at home and have a kip in the sun. Anyway, it'll be nice for Milly to get out into the bush for a while. She's spending far too much time indoors.'
Yeah, right, thought Millicent, remembering the long nightly excursions she was having around the neighbourhood. And it's *Millicent, thank you*! You may think I'm being lazy but what about the piles of dead mice I leave you almost every morning? You think Bertha's responsible for all that hunting? I need my rest during the day, girls.
But Millicent didn't really mind. Like all Oriental Shorthairs she loved human company and the attention she demanded. Anyway, out in the bush she would be able to catch up on the sleep she sorely needed while Pat and Jenny lay around having lunch, reading and resting.
And it's another chance to accustom myself to the area, and there might be a chance to pick up the odd bit of gossip and intelligence listening to Pat and Jenny, too, she mused.
She noticed that Pat had loaded the golf clubs in the back of the ute. Oh, it looks like we're off to the golf course, she thought, that'll be a nice change. Haven't seen the golf course: might be a few lizards to chase while they have a hit

around. Give the girls a bit of exercise, too. I hope they aren't intending to leave me locked in the ute in this heat. I'll fry!

But she needn't have worried. Pat and Jenny were very aware of the dangers of leaving pets locked in cars. They drove, as usual, with Millicent riding in the ute's cabin, perched on Jenny's shoulder where she could watch the road ahead and the passing scenery.

The country was beautiful and the bush grew exceptionally dense as they drove a short distance into the foothills. Millicent began to doze, hypnotised by the greenery and the warmth of the cabin, but, as always, her ears remained alert. It was just as well because it was during this part of the trip that she heard the name 'Victor Delmonte' mentioned. Her ears pricked up as she heard Pat telling Jenny that word around town had it that Delmonte, a reclusive but well-known and apparently prosperous businessman of the district, was rumoured to own the many acres of bushland they were passing through. It was also said that he had apparently been offered a fortune for the property for redevelopment but had steadfastly refused to sell claiming he wanted to preserve the natural bush and wild habitat. But Pat was of the opinion that it was for a far more sinister reason.

Delmonte, though hardly ever seen, had the reputation of a shrewd and hard-line businessman with few scruples and had sold various other properties with little regard for the environment. Millicent also noticed through the lush growth that there occasionally appeared to be a high barbed wire fence bordering the property. Pat and Jenny had never actually met the man but it seemed he had a fierce reputation and it was said that some of his hirelings were nothing short of thugs. Millicent checked the co-ordinates on her inner GPS and stored the information for further investigation.

Shortly afterwards they crossed a creek and came upon a small clearing where Pat pulled up and parked the ute. They got out and Millicent warily checked the area while Jenny retrieved the picnic basket, clubs and rug which she placed on the short-grassed area that bordered the creek. She then took the harness and extension lead from the glove box, clipped the harness over Millicent's head and shoulders, and attached the plastic handle of the extension lead to a tree stump.

Is this really necessary? Millicent sighed as she was forced to accept the restraining lead. I'm certainly not going to wander away and miss the chance of a lift back home. And where the hell are we, anyway? This doesn't look like a golf course, she thought, studying the wooded surroundings, unless we're parked just off the course and they're going to walk to the tee. Oh, well, this'll do me fine; there's some lovely soft grass to lie on in the shade where I can nibble or snooze, and the bloody lead will at least let me get to the creek for a drink if I need one.

But before she could quite get her bearings, Jenny walked over to the golf bag and said, 'Which iron do you think would be best?'

'I'd go for the four iron, it's got the heavier head,' Pat replied with a laugh.

Oh, they're just going to have a few practice shots, Millicent thought as she began to make her way toward the creek edge. They're sure to lose the ball in all this underbrush anyway.

'Now don't go too far, Milly,' Jenny called, as the restraining lead played out from the reel.

Millicent! she fumed to herself in exasperation. Will they *never* learn? And I will do exactly as I please, thank you, I'm a cat!

She carefully made her way down to the shallow creek edge to watch the crystal-clear water tumbling over the river stones and forming little ponds that reflected the clear blue sky. Tadpoles darted about playing hide and seek amongst the river stones. She dipped her paw into the slowly flowing water and withdrew it immediately. It was quite cold and although she had been through rigorous pool training at the Agency, which she had loathed, she and water didn't mix except under extreme life-threatening situations and the odd lap when she was thirsty.

The air conditioning in the ute's cabin had dehydrated her, so she took advantage of the opportunity and dipped her pink tongue into the water, preparing to drink heartily.

Suddenly, like a rifle shot, Millicent heard a loud *thwack*! She ducked instinctively as a blurred object shot over her head and landed on the other side of the creek.

'Good shot!' exclaimed Pat, 'but you sliced it a bit. Watch you don't hit Milly.'

Millicent! the infuriated furry one raged, and I'll go along with that. I do not need to be holed in one!

Millicent turned back from the water and crouched behind a log, out of danger, to watch the action. At that moment she was startled by a deep croak from nearby.

'Uh-oh, the hunters are out in full strength again.' The sound came from a large ugly brown frog crouched low almost under the log.

Millicent immediately hissed, spat, arched her back and assumed her *dori dachi* – defence stance, ready to protect herself.

'I wouldn't do that if I were you,' said the frog warningly, 'unless you'd like a mouthful of deadly poison.' He was puffing up the poisonous parotoid glands on his shoulders. 'One bite and I'd give you ten-fifteen minutes, tops.'

'Who are you?' Millicent hissed. 'Or rather, *what* are you? I've got to say I've seen some pretty ugly-looking frogs in my time but you take the catnip.'

'I'm not a frog, sweet-tooth, I'm a cane toad. You must be new around here. You never heard of cane toads?'

'Of course I have,' replied Millicent testily, 'it's just that I've never *seen* one. I'm from down south, you see, and we don't have any of you lot down there.'

'Yet,' croaked the toad. 'But give us time,' he added evilly, 'give us time. – Carny,' he croaked, 'That's my name, Carny Cane Toad. I'd shake hands but that might be a bit painful for you.' He studied her closely through his heavily hooded black eyes and chuckled.

She noticed he was quite different to the other frogs and toads she'd seen. His back feet had leathery webbing between the toes but his front feet actually had separate toes! And almost his entire body was covered with ugly warts. He was not a pretty sight. She had quite enjoyed the odd meal of frog's legs but this one was definitely not the attractively edible type. He certainly could do with the services of a beauty parlour and from her observations the town was desperately in need of one.

'And just what are you, my funny, furry little friend? I suppose you are a cat of some sort but you're not the general run-of-the-mill sort of cat, are you?'

'I most certainly am not,' replied Millicent haughtily. 'I am a pure-bred Oriental Shorthair, thank you very much, quite rare, and I'm sure we wouldn't move in the same social circles.'

'Oo-er,' sneered the toad, 'aren't we grand? I'd give you six weeks alone out here in the bush and you'd be just as ugly, or dead, as the other ferals that hang about and chase us. But they soon learn their lesson – a bit too late I can assure you.'

'Oh, there's another one,' cried Jenny.

There was another thwack and another mangled brown missile flew through the air and landed only a metre away, splayed out like a road kill. There followed a series of blows and Millicent could hear the bludgeoned toads thudding further away and into the underbrush.

'Well, I'd better be off,' croaked Carny. 'They're getting closer. If you're still around here at sundown, drop down by the creek. There'll be a huge orgy going on. Just follow the mating calls. Our sheilas can lay from eight thousand up to thirty-five thousand eggs at a time and they manage two clutches a year. Us blokes lay on a keg, have a bit of a croak and a dance and have a whale of a time fertilising them, I can tell you. Today a tadpole, tomorrow the world!'

He took off, hopping in short rapid leaps over the log but stupidly headed across open ground towards the bush.

Thwack!

'Got you, you ugly bastard!' said Pat in a victory yell.

Well, Carny, it looks like there'll be another cane toad less at the orgy tonight, Millicent smiled to herself as she made her way back to the picnic rug.

With the area suitably cleared of the offending cane toads, Jenny laid out the picnic lunch and Millicent suddenly had a distinct impression of the smell of meat! She slowly crept forward to investigate this now unusual phenomenon and discovered a yellow plastic bowl containing what looked suspiciously like beef mince! She sniffed the contents and, sure enough, her observations were correct.

'Just a little treat for you, Milly,' smiled Pat. 'Although we are against the principle of eating meat, this is a special occasion. You've been such a help to Bertha in controlling the mice, you're affectionate and you've become a definite asset to have around the place, hasn't she, Jen?'

'Yes, she's a real sweetie,' cooed Jenny, stroking Millicent's ears.

Millicent was quite moved by their kindness and basked in their attention. After all, it was always hard to get good staff nowadays. She squatted down contentedly and soon demolished the mince in eager gulps.

Naturally, although the meat was delicious on the way down, after so long she had become quite unused to the ingestion of real beef, so it wasn't long before her stomach revolted and she was forced to vomit most of the meal back up again. It was obviously just a little too rich after her diet of mice and vegetarian junk food.

'That'll teach you to gulp your food down,' laughed Pat, but Millicent wasn't amused as her stomach heaved.

They think I'm just being greedy, she thought, somewhat abashed, but really it's only a mild form of bulimia. A girl has to watch her figure, after all.

She sat and licked her paws and hindquarters to regain her composure and then settled down on the rug for a little snooze while Pat and Jenny lay on the grass to read. This is so peaceful, Millicent thought, as she drifted off to sleep to the burbling sounds of the river, the mating calls of cicadas and cane toads.

Suddenly she was awake, alerted to a strange slithering sound coming from the direction of the creek. Her eyes opened and with the slightest movement of her head she surveyed the direction from which the sound had come. She also noticed a strange, unpleasant odour drifting on the still air from the same direction. My God, she thought, as she spied a long slender reptile slithering toward the now sleeping staff, It's a snake! This bloody place is full of wildlife! Her fur bristled as she prepared herself for an assault, watching the reptile heading closer to the picnic rug. She must save Pat and Jenny from attack. They'd treated her so well and besides, who else would she have to drive her home?

The snake was different to any others she had encountered and was not recognisable from those she had studied in her training period. It was over a metre in length with a smallish, flat head, and its long, slim body was a greyish brown with a rather beautiful spotted and striped pattern in shades of green and grey. She could not identify if it was a venomous variety but she felt she couldn't take the chance with her and the staff's safety at risk.

She crouched and waited until the reptile came within range and sprang! She leapt high above the snake and landed on its back away from the head which immediately displayed a large gaping mouth filled with evil-looking fangs. She sank her claws into the snake's now slashing body and hung on. Both protagonists hissed and rolled and writhed for advantage but Millicent had the position away from its gaping jaws and with great agility fought desperately to drag the snake away from Pat and Jenny who had quickly awoken to the noise of the combat.

'Millicent! No!' cried Pat. 'Let it go! It's harmless! It's not venomous,' she yelled as she jumped to her feet and raced toward the writhing duo. Keeping well away from the snake's head, she grabbed Millicent's lead and suddenly jerked her away from the battle, quickly snatching the snake by the tail and holding it up. 'It's only a keelback – a swamp snake. It's harmless,' she said, as she held the still writhing reptile high in the air above Millicent. 'They only eat tadpoles and frogs but more importantly, they're one of the few snakes that can eat cane toads without being affected by their poison. They're very useful.'

By now Jenny had joined them and studied the snake intently, wrinkling her nose at the unpleasant smell emanating from the creature. 'They fart, you know – when they're distressed.'

'What?' roared Pat, raucously. 'I was blaming Millicent for the smell.'

Millicent was aghast at this insensitive remark, slitting her eyes and twitching her tail to demonstrate her disapproval.

'Yes, I was only reading about them a couple of days ago,' Jenny continued. 'They're not very common this far south. It must have been washed down in the last floods. We could do with a few more of them around here to fight the cane toad plague. It said in this article that they seem to have evolved quite quickly over the last thirty-odd years so that their bodies are longer but their heads and their jaws have remained relatively small so they can only swallow small toads and not absorb as much venom. It was fascinating.'

'Well, aren't you becoming the little herpetologist,' laughed Pat. 'Come on, little fellow,' she said as she carried the snake back to the creek and slipped it back into the water, 'off you go.'

The snake quickly swam away upstream and disappeared into a pile of logs that had been washed down the creek and jammed against the bank, no doubt thanking its lucky stars, or maybe Warrajum, the ancient Rainbow Serpent who protected the area, particularly it being a creature of the same kind.

Millicent quickly regained her composure and trotted back towards the ute dismissing the whole incident.

Well, how was I to know? she brooded defensively. I'm from the south. How am I supposed to tell the difference between a venomous and a non-venomous snake? A snake is a snake. Better to be sure than sorry. Bloody sub-tropical wildlife, she muttered as she stalked under the ute and lay down in the shade.

Pat and Jenny sang as they drove back towards the town. Millicent decided she quite liked the sound of their voices singing to the strains of 'Naughty Girls Need Love Too' – an 80s hit by Samantha Fox, and 'I'll Always Love You' by Taylor Dayne, above the purring of the engine. But when they belted out, 'Need You Tonight', the INXS hit, she felt this was going a bit too far even for her tolerant attitude.

There is a time and a place, girls, she reflected somewhat piously.

Chapter 7

Bertha was up and awake when they returned and the sun was slipping below the horizon, pulling the pink and gold rays with it and leaving lavender and mauve hues over the countryside.

'Well,' she said, 'you missed a bit of excitement while you were out gallivanting in the country. Reg next door and his two dopey sons had visitors today.'

'Oh, who?' asked Millicent.

'No names, no pack drill,' Bertha commented mysteriously, 'but there was a hell of a ruckus going on over there. Lots of shouting and language I haven't heard since I was a stowaway in the Merchant Navy.' She stopped, lost in the memories of those exciting years sailing to the Orient and beyond. 'Did I ever tell you about the tabby tom and the nights in the lifeboat?'

'No,' sighed Millicent, reluctant to encourage the erotic details of Bertha's long-lost love life, 'but tell me exactly what happened at Binthere-Dunthat.'

'Oh, he was *gorgeous,*' purred Bertha, ignoring Millicent's question. 'We used to escape down the berthing ropes and visit all the exotic ports. We'd explore the tiny little alleyways and creep into shops and restaurants for late suppers.'

'You were lucky the both of you didn't wind up *being* the late suppers,' Millicent thought, having heard the most dreadful stories of what went into Oriental cooking.

Bertha gave a wheezing giggle, quite unaware of Millicent's interjection. 'The rubbish bins were simply loaded with delicious titbits. I do like Chinese cooking, don't you?

Oh, but of course you would, being Oriental yourself. And Tarquin was *so* protective.'

'Tarquin?' repeated Millicent, inquisitive in spite of herself.

'The tabby tom – Tarquin, that was his name,' Bertha explained patiently, his romantic image flooding her somewhat addled memory. 'He was named after one of the Etruscan kings apparently. I think he was the one who ravished Lucretia, Not my Tarquin, another one,' she quickly explained. 'The Roman matron killed herself rather than live with the shame. Silly woman; it would never have occurred to me to kill myself because Tarquin jumped me.' Again came the coy, wheezing giggle. 'I would've been suicidal all the time.'

'But Reg and the boys, Bertha,' Millicent persisted, patiently trying to bring Bertha back on track, 'what actually happened?'

'What?' replied Bertha, vaguely. 'Oh, yes.' She dragged her meandering memory back to the present. 'Well, like I said, they had visitors, two or three blokes in black outfits, driving black cars – heavies by the look of them. I think I heard a couple of gunshots. I'm not exactly sure; it could've just been my ears popping. They've been giving me a bit of a problem lately. I was sitting on the roof and heights tend to do that to me.' She paused to reconsider if it was actually shots she had heard but failed to come up with a definite answer. 'Anyway, the three blokes – or was it four? – my eyes aren't as good as they used to be either. Anyway, they took off in a bit of a hurry and it went quiet again. That's all I could see from the roof.'

Millicent contemplated a little sojourn over to Binthere-Dunthat to check it out but Jenny arrived out on the verandah with their dinner so she decided to leave it until later on when it was darker.

But after she'd crunched down the dried biscuits and washed them down with a little water from her bowl, she was a little sleepy so it was some time before she could investigate the matter further. As she dozed, lulled by the meal and the day's adventures, she slowly became aware of the distinct odour of smoke in the relatively still air.

'Where's that smell coming from, Bertha? Have Pat and Jenny lit the open fire in the living room?'

'What smell?' replied Bertha sniffing wetly. 'I can't smell anything with my sinuses in the state they're in.'

But Millicent had already spied the column of smoke rising from the direction of the neighbouring farm and taken off at great speed to investigate. She loped through the plants and underbrush at full pelt and jumped the high wire fence in time to see the farmhouse bursting into flames.

The fire was spreading quickly through the back of the old wooden building and she could see Reg and his two sons running around furiously trying to contain the blaze with garden hoses and buckets of water from the water tank. The smell of burning timber mixed with the unmistakable smell of cannabis was strong in the air and far in the distance she could hear the siren of the local fire authority truck, obviously alerted to the imminent danger of a bush fire.

She drew closer to watch the drama unfold but stayed far enough away not to be affected by the heat from the blaze. Her eyes began to water from the smoke and she began to feel incredibly light-headed. Then through the grey swirling smoke she was shocked to see King trying to escape from the back of the outhouse where he had saved her from the giant rat! To her horror she saw the flames engulf the roof and the supporting beams and with a crash the flaming old wooden rafters collapsed and fell to the ground in an explosion of sparks. King had disappeared from sight. With no thought for her own safety she leapt to his rescue, streaking toward the blaze in panic.

Oh, Goddess Bastet, she pleaded, save him – please save him! She ducked and weaved her way through the smoke and flickering flames to where she had last seen him. There he is! She suddenly saw his inert body lying on the ground beside a smouldering beam that had obviously hit him. Without taking time to examine his condition, she grabbed him by the scruff of the neck and began dragging him back and away from the flames that had now caught the dry grass and weeds by the path.

Summoning incredible strength and determination brought about by the fear for his safety, and no doubt from the inhalation of the dope-fuelled smoke, she managed to drag King well away from the blaze, toward the fence, out of harm's way. She glanced back at the fire and could have sworn she saw misty silhouettes running away through the cloud of smoke.

The already masked volunteer fire fighters arrived with the clamour of sirens and with disciplined action began unwinding hoses and extinguishing the inferno. But it was too late to save most of the ancient, tinder-dry structure and the back part of the dwelling and the outhouses were completely destroyed. Reg and his sons were singed and exhausted but saved from a disastrously painful death. But it was obvious from their shouting, wild gestures and abusive language they were far from happy.

The fire fighters eventually got the blaze under control and removed their masks, gradually relaxing, sitting, or lying on the grass, inhaling the smoke-filled air, giggling or chuckling, their eyes seemingly focused on some faraway object or distant thought which they were desperately trying to grasp. Soon their conversation became slower and deeper; delving into fanciful subjects in which they would not normally indulge. Gradually, even Reg and his boys calmed down and joined in the drug-induced group experience and soon there was a definite party mood in the congregation of men around the smouldering ruins of the buildings. A giggling Jacko appeared from the relatively undamaged front of the house carrying a large plastic bin containing several bottles of beer which he distributed amongst the men, and the party raged on.

Millicent carefully checked King's condition and placed her nose close to his mouth, relieved to find he was still breathing and apparently uninjured apart from a sizeable lump on his head. She sat watching him, waiting for him to recover, and in her heightened state of mind, his beauty seemed even more exquisite than she'd first realised. His rich brown coat shone like silk in the pale moonlight, his whiskers were divine and for the first time she noticed the delicate pale pink shade of his inner ears touched by the pale moonlight, seemingly almost deliciously transparent. His closed eyes were a slightly slanted line of black fur. His sleek tail now lay curled out behind him like a sensual serpent. His thighs were magnificently muscled under the radiant fur and her eyes meandered on …

Oh, she suddenly noticed in amazement, he's been neutered! Why would anyone do that? He'd have been wonderful for breeding! Her eyes were then drawn to the tiny metal zip clasp usually hidden beneath his lustrous stomach fur that concealed the mysterious pouch. This, with the addition of the separated claws on his paws, indeed only added to his mystery.

Tentatively she carefully reached her front paw out to slip a claw into the eyelet of the zipper intending to open the intriguing pouch and see what it concealed. Suddenly his front paw swung down, clamping her paw to his stomach, defeating her inquisitive action.

'Uh-uh,' he said, almost playfully, 'mustn't touch, cheeky puss.'

She quickly withdrew her paw and turned the movement into a licking motion as if cleaning her back leg. He smiled at her in that devilish way and she immediately felt she had to justify her intrusion. 'Oh, you're awake. I was just checking for any possible injury you may have sustained. You seem to be fine.'

'Just a slight bump on the head and a bit singed but otherwise everything seems to be in working order.'

Well, not quite everything, apparently, she thought, glancing at his castration scar. She turned to look back at the still glowing and smoking embers of the fire. A few tiny orange, red and blue sparks spat and flew into the air appearing like little sparkling insects escaping into the darkness. Somehow the scene fascinated her and she marvelled at the colours, smells and sounds like a symphony of the senses.

King suddenly giggled and struggled to control it. It quite surprised her as she would never have thought of him as a giggling type. Although she tried hard to suppress it she found herself joining in and soon they were both rolling on the ground in inexplicable laughter. 'I think maybe we were too close to the smoke,' King giggled, 'but hey, what the hell.'

They continued to roll around in merriment but the ridiculousness of the moment gradually passed and he lay on his side watching her and paused while Millicent fought to regain her composure. 'What on earth were you doing out here again, anyway?' she asked.

He took a long moment to study her before he replied. 'I had some further checking to do,' he said.

'Checking? On what?'

'The amount of stock they were holding in reserve,' he replied.

'And why would that interest you?' she asked.

He took a long moment to answer. 'How well can I trust you?' he asked, suddenly serious.

'I saved your life, remember?' she replied.

'True,' he said, thoughtfully.

He suddenly appeared to come to a decision and slowly reached for the zip on his pouch and opened it. 'I have to ask you to keep what I am about to show you, top secret,' he said conspiratorially.

'Of course,' she breathed, intrigued by his sudden change of manner.

He reached into his pouch and produced an ID card and showed it to her. 'King Burma', it said on the card and underneath, 'Agent of the FBI'.

'FBI?' Millicent queried, in shock.

'Feline Bureau of Investigation,' he nodded seriously.

Millicent gasped and then gave a huge ironic sigh. 'I might've guessed it,' she said. 'The Agencies never trust each other enough to actually communicate and share intelligence with each other, do we?'

'We?' he asked.

'Princess Millicent Srirasmi,' she responded. 'CIA – Cat Intelligence Agency.'

He roared with laughter. 'No, I don't believe it!'

'Well, it's true,' she said. 'It looks like we've been sent on the same mission. What a waste of funding.'

'That's political budgeting for you,' he shrugged. 'It happens in all the departments. So, you're here to investigate the drug trade?'

'Yep,' she said, flicking her tail as she rose, moving away a few paces.

'What have you got so far?' he asked.

'Not much,' she replied, disheartened. 'I've only been here a short while and it's taken me time to find a base, establish my cover story and settle in. But that's all taken care of so I intend progressing faster now. How about you?'

'Oh, I've been here for a long time but I still haven't been able to get to the top guys. Quite a few leads but nothing concrete. This lot tonight will stir things up a bit and maybe I'll find the crack I'm looking for.'

'*We're* looking for,' she corrected.

He smiled. *'We?* Okay. What say we pool our resources and see if we can get the job done? Maybe we can get it over with and move on. I'm getting a bit tired of working undercover as a hippy cat.'

'I hate to tell you,' Millicent smiled, 'but a *hippy* cat you ain't.'

'What do you mean?' King replied, taking offence. 'I'm a vegetarian, well mostly, and I never bathe.'

'It's going to take more than that,' she smiled. 'You're far too – classy.'

'Well, there's the pot-sniffing Princess calling the kettle black,' he retorted. 'Anyway, what about a little collusion?'

'Oh, you men are all alike – one-track mind.'

'I meant with the investigation.'

'Oh,' she said, a little rebuked. 'I'll think about it,'

She paused, weighing up the pros and cons and decided that maybe two cats' heads were probably better than one. 'Let's go and catch ourselves a bit of supper and I'll think about it. I don't know why but I'm suddenly starving.'

'Right on, Princess, I've a touch of the munchies myself,' King grinned as together they made their way back towards the chicken coop. 'I'll tell you what I've discovered so far …'

King related to her how he had set up a network of informers throughout the district. Being located at the vet clinic had its advantages. He came into contact with many of the patients and, being very charming and gregarious in nature, he was able to obtain important information from a wide assortment of animals. The locals' pets were very susceptible. For example he'd even befriended a number of dogs who could sniff out information, which gave him a very diverse perspective on the activities of the area. Sadly, the dogs of course mostly saw their roles as servants and confidants of their masters as opposed to the cats, who knew their positions were completely reversed, but King managed to charm himself into the confidence of the canines who visited the clinic by appearing subservient and a little naive; a role he found extremely difficult to achieve with his intelligence and innate sense of superiority. But he was a very experienced and talented agent, well trained in the art of skilful deception.

There was a forlorn-looking part-Afghan called Arthur, who had inherited the sub-intelligence of what many dog observers claim as the number one least intelligent breed. King flattered and had convinced the scrawny long-legged hound that he was clever and of superior intellect. This had been a major achievement as Arthur had displayed a very unfriendly attitude on their first encounter and barked ferociously. King had completely disregarded the show of bravado and clawed open a packet of dried dog food and surreptitiously fed Arthur a few crumbs in exchange for information. Arthur was a sucker for a treat or two.

Barney was a Bloodhound with a deep furrowed frown and folds of skin that almost caused his eyes and character to disappear completely to become just a blob of hair. But he was useful for his ability to sniff out and follow suspects. He was an instinctive sniffer and also responded well to bribes of food, but he had to be restrained when pet rabbits attended the surgery.

King had recruited other cats, mostly inbred, common varieties that immediately recognised him as the alpha leader and took orders obediently. But he had failed with a few; one example had been a young moggie, Mahitabelle, with a bad case of separation anxiety, caused by the rest of the litter being drowned at birth. 'Why me?' she meowed plaintively. 'Why was I the only one to survive?' Despite counselling from King and many courses of anti-depressant drugs, courtesy of Dr Fellini, Mahitabelle failed to respond and eventually ran away into the bush to become a wild cat to escape from her trauma. This had not been a wise move as eventually she was kicked by a cassowary and died a painful death.

Chapter 8

'What do you think was the purpose behind the attack on Binthere-Dunthat?' Millicent asked King a few days later when Pat and Jenny had taken her to town for a spot of shopping. They had fortunately left her tethered to a bench outside the vet's surgery where she could climb on the backrest if danger threatened. King had spied her arrival and soon joined her.

'Standover tactics, I would expect,' replied King confidently. 'The big guys were giving Reg and the boys a warning not to cross them or get any ideas of going solo or expanding their business.'

'But they were only a small concern as far as I could tell,' opined Millicent.

King shrugged and began to lick his back. 'There were shots fired earlier in the afternoon,' he said. 'I heard them. I reckon our Reggie, or one of his hoon sons, fired a couple of shots to scare off the competition and it backfired. Not a good idea to mess with the big boys.'

'But who are they, these *big boys*?'

King shrugged. 'Can't seem to get a handle on that yet.'

'Bertha said she thought she'd heard shots too, but how did you hear the shots from so far away?'

'Oh, I was just out for a stroll,' he replied with a wink.

Millicent told him of her adventures on the picnic, which amused him, but when she related the information she'd picked up about the suspected Victor Delmonte drug connection, his attitude changed markedly.

'Ah,' he purred, 'that's interesting. That name has come up a few times lately. I've never actually had contact with Mr

Delmonte, he seems to be a bit of a mystery man, but Barney let slip that he'd heard there were a couple of vicious Rottweilers kept on guard at one of his properties. They've never been brought into the surgery but I think Dr Fellini has been called out a couple of times to treat them – you know, house calls. I'll take a look at the records.'

'Well, I have the map co-ordinates of this property stored on my microchip, if that's any help.'

'Indeed it is,' replied King enthusiastically. 'It could be worthwhile taking a little trip out there to have a look around.'

But before any further discussion could take place, Pat and Jenny arrived back and King retreated back into the surgery with a flick of his tail.

Bertha was asleep as usual when they returned to the farm so Millicent joined Pat and Jenny in the vegetable plot. She loved the smells of the earth and the vegetables as they were picked and packed into the crates to be collected for the market. The local market was always a delight for Millicent. Although she was restrained by that bloody harness, she was always tethered in the shade with a bowl of water nearby. There was a festive mood with stall holders and buyers milling around. It also gave Millicent the chance to study the locals and tourists and pick up the odd bit of conversation and local colour. Nobody takes any notice of a cat curled up apparently asleep.

Some of the locals were indeed colourful and strange with their second-hand, or hand-woven, homemade garments, funny hats and out-of-date shoes in contrast with the more conservatively dressed tourists. And some of the hairstyles intrigued her; many plaits and dreadlocks that somehow reminded her of dead reptiles or strings of dried dog excrement hanging down their backs. Why would humans do that to themselves? she wondered. Tattoos were also a pet dislike, so to speak, of hers and there were many on display:

snakes and butterflies and naked bodies and intricate patterns in blues, black and greens. She even noticed a white Birman-cross whose luxuriant fur, dyed in vivid colours to form a walking work of art, had its ears and legs shaved into intricate shapes and patterns to give it a Salvador Dali appearance. Its naturally white feet had been dyed blue! How embarrassing, Millicent thought with a sneer. Some humans have no respect for an animal's dignity. By the scrunched look on the Birman's face, it obviously agreed with her although it was hard to tell with Birmans whose faces were always scrunched anyway.

Her eye was drawn to a particularly scruffy-looking old man wearing tartan pants, a grubby green-striped shirt, a battered old silk tie and a hat that looked for all the world like a rather sloppy cowpat. On his feet he wore blue rubber thongs. It wasn't his appearance that caught her attention but the beautiful, slim, young dark-haired girl with him. She was dressed in a long, flowing, silk floral skirt with a pale pink blouse, open at the neck, provocatively displaying the curves of smooth tanned breasts, with a single blue butterfly design tattooed high on one side near her long slender throat. Her unusually clean feet were shod in delicately strapped gold sandals. She laughed gaily at something the old man said and the sound reminded Millicent of the creek water tumbling over the rocks. She was quite exquisite – for a human. But it was the contrast of the two that took Millicent's attention. 'Beauty and the beast' suddenly flashed into her mind. If this was father and daughter the beautiful young maiden had fortunately inherited her looks from her mother's gene pool. If it was a sexual relationship, the old man certainly had the better deal.

The girl handed a small brown paper package to the stall keeper and in return, received a delicate silver necklace inset with a small purple amethyst, surrounded by what looked like tiny sparkling diamonds. She handed the purple tissue-papered package to the old man who immediately stowed it in the large brown leather carry bag at his feet. The necklace would match perfectly with the small diamond studs the girl wore in her ear lobes, Millicent decided. As far as she could tell, she also noticed that no money actually exchanged hands during the transaction and pondered the implications: A gift perhaps? A trade? A barter?

She continued to watch as the couple moved away, the young woman in the lead with the old man following closely behind, They headed for a shiny black SUV parked in the area reserved for vehicles. A young, thick-set, muscular man sat waiting at the wheel and when the couple approached, he jumped out of the car, opened the back passenger door and the young woman climbed in. The old man joined the driver in the front passenger seat, the motor roared into life and the car sped off.

King had been busy. He'd checked the files and found the information he was looking for. He found the reference to Victor Delmonte under 'Ralph and Rudy Rottweiler' – owner, Mr Victor Delmonte. He compared the address to the co-ordinates Millicent had given him and didn't find a match. This did not surprise him but Dr Fellini's handwritten note in the margin did. Apparently Ralph and Rudy had a police record! They'd been taken into custody on three occasions for 'disturbing the peace' and for viciously attacking Mick and Jacko Morrison, Reg's two sons. Evidence of a feud? Mr Delmonte had been charged with failing to keep his dogs under control but mysteriously the charges had later been dropped after compensation had been paid to Reg.

King checked with his informants in the police department but little seemed to be known about the mysterious Mr Delmonte. He couldn't even get a description. He decided he would personally carry out a reconnaissance on the Delmonte property.

'Bertha,' Millicent asked her friend who was taking a pee in the kitty litter tray, 'do you know anything about a Victor Delmonte?'

Bertha raised her head languidly and stared at Millicent for some time while she concentrated on her ablutions before she replied, 'Victor Delmonte? Not much. He's not seen around a lot apparently. I've heard he's got a pair of vicious Rottweilers; they live on a property on the other side of town, only moved into the area a couple of years ago.'

'What does he do? I mean, is it a dairy, or does he run cattle, or maybe a banana plantation?'

Bertha shrugged her shoulders which caused her to wince as she stepped out of the tray and gave a perfunctory and unsatisfactory scratch at the litter. 'Ouch, bloody rheumatism. Why do you want to know?'

'Oh, no particular reason,' Millicent replied distractedly. 'His name came up the other day when we were out on the picnic. They say he's very rich and owns a lot of property around here.'

'Wouldn't know,' groaned Bertha, as she limped back out through the pet flap and settled into a more comfortable position on the back deck. 'I've heard he's got a beautiful daughter who causes a lot of attention around town when she shows up: very different type to the locals. Looks more like a city girl – model looks, apparently, dresses in designer labels, would you believe. Pisses off the scarecrow sheilas around the place I'll bet, even if they won't admit it.'

'Wonder why they live out here?' Millicent mused out loud. 'Hardly sound the type.'

'It takes all kinds,' Bertha sighed, closing her one good eye which gave the impression she was winking. 'Maybe she's disillusioned and wants to get away from the glamorous city life – usual story around here. Who knows?'

'Pat and Jenny around?' Millicent asked, changing the subject abruptly.

'Down the paddock,' Bertha yawned and replied sleepily.

Millicent stretched languidly and made her way through the pet flap back into the house. She went directly to the office and jumped up on the computer and logged onto the secure internet address. *'Tom – See what you can dig up on a Victor Delmonte: moved here a couple of years ago. No background available.'* She tapped the 'Send' icon.

It wasn't long before she heard the ping signalling incoming mail. She opened the file and read, *'Victor Delmonte – one of the aliases for Robert Lyons – never convicted but mentioned several times in drug-related offenses. Disappeared two years ago – destination unknown. Considered dangerous – possibly murdered. Will forward mug shot. Take care – keep up the good work. – Tom.'*

Suddenly she heard Jenny arriving in the kitchen to get lunch. Millicent quickly deleted the message, exited the program and sat for a moment staring at the blank screen. She then climbed onto the keyboard and curled up, pretending to be asleep.

'Oh, there you are, you sleepy girl,' Jenny said, entering the office. 'I suppose you've been hard at work on the computer writing your autobiography,' she chuckled.

If you only knew, thought Millicent, yawning as if awoken from a deep sleep.

'Come on, off the keyboard, cheeky,' said Jenny, lifting Millicent into her arms. 'You cats pick the darndest places to sleep.'

'Well, I need all the rest I can get,' Millicent meowed, 'I've got a big night in front of me.'

Chapter 9

After dinner, when the daylight was fading into a pink and purple twilight, Millicent escaped through the cat flap, leaving Bertha preparing to settle down on Pat's lap to watch a silly film about an animated mouse, and took off on her long journey. She'd recalled the map co-ordinates from her GPS and retraced the route they'd taken on their way to the picnic, using all the skills she had learned at the Academy. She took advantage of as much natural cover as she could, kept low and moved fast as if being stalked by a predator. She kept away from the main road and opted for the more direct route, moving swiftly through paddocks of cattle and bush. At one stage she disturbed a clutch of rabbits, who panicked and skipped off in a zig-zag direction back to their warren. Her mind, although strictly focused on her objective, wandered back to gentler times when she sat in the Canberra sun reading *Watership Down* and wondered if the local bunnies too were worried about the destruction of their warren and the social implications.

She came upon many creeks and the mating calls of cane toads almost deafened her. She thought back to Carny and his sudden and unexpected departure from the orgy club scene and wondered if he had survived the very different sort of clubbing. Somehow she doubted it.

Soon darkness settled in and with her excellent night vision, she felt safer and more confident to increase her speed.

Eventually she reached her objective and slowed down as she approached the barbed wire fence she had noted from the ute's cabin. Her heart rate soon returned to normal as her respiratory system was in excellent condition and she was relieved she hadn't invited the consumptive Bertha to join her on this excursion. Carefully picking her way through the lethal barbs she entered the danger zone.

She made her way through dense undergrowth and thick stands of trees, ever on guard against the unexpected. She noticed several snakes which she identified as venomous and gave them a wide berth. Now was not the time to be foolhardy. Lizards and insects were also out in full force on their nightly hunting expeditions but she ignored them and continued deeper into the forbidden zone.

Presently, she heard men's voices and crouched to take stock of her situation. Through the underbrush she saw the red glow of a small campfire with six men silhouetted against the flickering flames. They each carried a can of what she supposed was beer and were absorbed in their meal of barbecued meat as they chatted. The smell was intoxicating but she fought against the temptation of joining them. There were several tents nearby, their flaps open to the night air; some with gas lamps lighting the interior but there were still enough shadows to afford her sufficient cover.

Using the shadows and clumps of grass for concealment, she slithered her way forward and suddenly stopped. Resting against a fallen tree trunk she saw several rifles well within easy reach of the men. Now this added a further complication to her survival if she were discovered. These men might easily be hunters, of course, but this was of little consolation if she suddenly became the prey. Carefully she skirted the camp and came across a large shed that stood in darkness except for a small gas lamp by the entrance. She was about to enter to investigate the contents when she suddenly heard the sound of a truck engine approaching along a rough pebbled path which led to the shed. She darted into the shed and hid herself in a corner behind a forklift tractor.

The vehicle came to a stop and she heard the slam of car doors followed by the crunching sound of approaching boots. Suddenly the interior of the shed became ablaze with lights and she peeked from her hiding place to see a slim young man, wearing overalls and a beanie covering most of his head, with his hand resting on a series of light switches. There was more crunching of boots and the men, she presumed from the campfire, entered.

'Right, to work!' the young man ordered in the manner of an army drill sergeant as he strode toward a door at the end of the building, unlocked it with a key from his pocket, and entered. The men followed wordlessly, leaving the door ajar. Millicent, taking advantage of any available cover, crept toward the door and peeked in. The room looked like a scientific laboratory with shelves, a central table and various pieces of technical equipment placed around the room. Millicent could just make out the names of some of the chemicals stored on the shelves; dilute sulphuric acid, Potassium Permanganate and Hydrogen Peroxide.

In hessian bags stacked against the wall Millicent could see sprigs of leaves about five centimetres long, with red berries attached. A few held single or pairs of white petal flowers with the red berries beginning to form. My God, she thought, they're coca leaves! They're growing coca and manufacturing cocaine! Tom was right, there's more than marijuana being grown around here. Weed is one thing but cocaine is a completely different kettle of fish.

In her ear she heard a soft whisper. '*Erythroyxlum novogranatense* genus – the coca plant – not to be confused with *Erythroyxlum australe* which is natural to Australia – particularly to New South Wales. This is the Southern American genus – very potent and very illegal. Must smuggle the seeds in. Well, well, well, a cocaine factory right on the doorstep.'

Millicent attempted to spin around to face the whisperer but his paws held her tight.

'Steady, steady, my little Princess. Keep very still.'

Millicent froze in his hold. 'King?' she whispered back.

'Right on, Princess. I suggest we very carefully back out of here. You've seen all you need to see at the moment. Time for a confab.'

She nodded and they both began to edge their way out. Just as they reached the exit door they were suddenly met with a low, evil growl. The two Rottweilers, Ralph and Randy, stood facing them, their eyes cold and hard, their jaws open to reveal lethal fangs dripping with saliva, every muscle tensed for action. Millicent and King froze to the spot.

The maddened guard dogs suddenly barked fiercely and lunged forward. Fortunately for Millicent and King the hounds came to a sudden stop inches away from them but still continued barking furiously. They were chained to the truck a few feet away and had reached the end of their restraint.

'Oops, time to take off, I think, Princess.'

They sprang as one away from the enraged dogs and, at full speed, they headed for the bush and raced toward the fence, careless of the branches, leaves and twigs that slashed in their wake. Behind them they heard shouting from the men mixed with the livid barking of the dogs, followed by the unmistakable sounds of gunfire. The shots ricocheted off nearby trees and rocks but their aim was high, the men fearing that they had been targeted by other humans.

'Probably only a roo,' said one of the men.

Millicent and King hurled themselves over the fence paying no heed to the razor sharp prongs, and headed back along the road.

'No,' cried Millicent, 'this way! It's a shortcut!'

She left the road and led the way back along the track she had used to get there. King fell dutifully in behind. After about a kilometre she stopped and waited for King to catch up. 'What the hell were you doing out there?' she asked.

'I might ask you the same question,' replied King. 'You might at least have invited me along. We are, after all, on the same side.'

'I was just reconnoitring, 'she said. 'I fully intended reporting back to you next time we met.'

'I'll bet,' King retorted, doubtfully,

'Oh, have it your own way, King. This is not solely your investigation, you know.'

'I thought we were *partners*,' he replied with just a hint of sarcasm.

'I have an assignment and I intend carrying it through.'

He stopped, forcing her to turn to him. 'This is bigger than either of us expected. We thought we were just after the cannabis dealers.'

'I didn't,' she replied. 'Who cares about a bit of dope being smoked by the locals? I'm after the big boys.'

'Well, I think we might've found them, Princess. What are you planning for your next step – closing them down single handed?'

'I'm working on it,' she replied smugly.

'We've got to find out where they're cultivating the coca crop, for a start.'

'And then what? We going to set fire to it? Get real, King. Or do you have a stash of gelignite tucked away in your pouch?'

'I'm working on it,' he replied, mimicking the tone she had used.

She flicked her tail and continued on her way.

There was the usual exchange of emails with Canberra and Tom congratulated Millicent on her progress. She hadn't mentioned King as she thought that piece of information would best be kept secret at this stage until she saw how things played out. Tom was excited about her discovering the cocaine production location and said he would check it out and get back to her when a decision had been made on what further action should be taken. In the meantime she was to send the map co-ordinates of the property and keep her eyes and ears open and inform him of any further developments.

With this in mind she decided to draw Bertha out in idle conversation and learn if she had any information that could be usable. She subtly approached the subject with Bertha over the water bowl.

'So what do you think about the fire over at Binthere-Dunthat the other night?'

Bertha paused in her lapping and looked up at her with trickles of water dripping from her whiskers and chin. She wiped them off with her paw before she replied. 'It was a set-up, that's for sure.'

'By whom?' Millicent asked innocently.

Bertha shrugged and limped away to sit on the doormat. 'I told you I heard gunshots coming from there in the afternoon. Well, I reckon whoever Reg and the boys scared off came back and set fire to the place later on – as a warning.'

'Arson?' Millicent cried in mock disbelief. 'But who would do such a thing? I mean, it wasn't as if they were big dope suppliers – were they?'

Bertha gave her a shrewd look. 'Why share the market when you can have it all? I mean, let's face it, there are dozens of small operators around the district and they all have to pay protection. It goes with the territory.'

'Protection? There's a protection racket going on in the trade? Who's running it?'

Millicent couldn't be sure if Bertha winked or if it was just her funny eye twitching. She shrugged. 'Ah, it's not like the old days,' sighed Bertha. 'Everyone who wanted to grow their own supply – just small crops, y'know, sort of hobby farming – just went about it. But nowadays, the big demand is there so the dealers have moved in from the city. And some of them are bad bastards.'

'But you don't know who?"

Bertha shrugged again, bringing another frown of pain to her face.

'So you're in favour of people growing and smoking weed for their own use?' Millicent persisted.

Bertha looked at her as if she was mad. 'What?' she almost spat out. 'You forget I belong to Pat and Jenny.' Millicent tactfully ignored the 'belonging' bit. 'They're dead against any drugs. This has always been a strictly dope-free environment. I used to listen to their horror stories while I sat on their laps and they drank their chamomile tea and watched the tele. They've had a few bad experiences, I can tell you. Their parents were full-on druggies and they moved from cannabis onto the hard stuff and the kids had a terrible time; no money for food or decent clothes, ignored, abused, cop raids, parents jailed – you name it, they experienced it. It sort of puts you off any tolerance of any drug.' She paused in her tirade and then sighed. 'I know where all the secret crops are and if I was younger and had my way I'd root the whole lot out.'

'Would you?' Millicent asked seriously, staring directly into Bertha's good eye.

'Too right,' replied Bertha.

'Well, why don't we? I mean, we must be able to work out some way of destroying the crops.'

'Huh!' Bertha scoffed, 'it'd take years. And I don't dig so well anymore you may have noticed. I can just manage the litter tray. Well, that's not the only reason I have to use the tray,' she continued. 'I used to go in the garden but my pee killed off the vegies.' There was a long pause while Bertha considered how best to explain her unusual condition. 'You see,' she said, almost reluctantly, 'I have this – well, kidney problem – highly acidic or something. I wiped out a whole bed of strawberries once. I can tell you Pat and Jenny were not amused. So, I was relegated to the dreaded pet litter tray. I can't tell you how many whacks with a rolled up newspaper I suffered until I got into the habit.'

But Millicent had stopped listening for a moment while the information sank in.

'You mean your urine is poisonous to plants – all plants?'

'Pretty much,' Bertha admitted, reluctantly. 'Mind you, I'm not alone in that. I know of dozens of cats whose pee is lethal.'

'From around the district?' Millicent persisted.

'Yeah, of course. Don't tell me your pee is as pure as the falling rain.'

'Well, I've never actually taken any notice,' Millicent replied thoughtfully, 'but I'd be willing to give it a go.'

'What do you mean?' Bertha asked incredulously, 'you're not going to test it on Pat and Jenny's beetroot?'

'No, of course not,' Millicent replied, 'but I do know a crop very close we could try it out on.'

Bertha looked at her questioningly.

'Reg's cannabis! We could both give it a go at Binthere-Dunthat!'

'That's a pretty big crop,' Bertha replied doubtfully.

Millicent smiled and pushed the water bowl over to Bertha. 'Drink up, Bertha, we've got a mission to accomplish.'

Chapter 10

That night they furtively made their way to the next-door farm, being careful to avoid the guard dogs that roamed the area. This necessitated Millicent occasionally climbing one of the Eucalyptus trees and scouting the area. During one of these excursions she surprised a possum enjoying a fruit supper who, getting such a surprise at being confronted by Millicent, promptly let out a squawk, clutched its chest dramatically and went into an impromptu death scene that would really have done Al Pacino justice; twisting and writhing with such fervour, it promptly fell off the branch and almost landed on a rather surprised Bertha who was waiting below. You may not know this but possums involuntarily emit a dreadful smell when threatened by a predator and the stench was certainly enough to clear Bertha's sinus.

'Whew!' exclaimed Bertha. 'That possum has a bad flatulence problem!'

'Ignore it,' Millicent stated, unimpressed. 'It's just playing dead. They do that. They're *so* over-dramatic – real little drama queens.'

Sure enough, the possum suddenly revived, stood on its hind legs with hands on hips, deeply offended at the criticism of its performance, gave a 'Humph' of disgust and stalked off.

'All's clear,' called Millicent as she descended, 'the dogs are flat out asleep down the side of the house.' She and Bertha crept through the chicken wire fence into the tomato bed and headed directly to the cannabis plants.

'Quick!' muttered Bertha. 'Which one? I'm busting for a pee.'

'That one,' indicated Millicent, directing Bertha to the first cannabis plant in the row. 'See if you can manage more than one.'

'No problemo,' sighed Bertha as she relieved her bladder in a stream that would have done credit to a fire hose.

Millicent attempted to follow suit but her bladder was less full and could only manage a short squirt. Bertha's aim was admirable and managed to target three cannabis plants successfully but accidently hit two tomatoes when she was checking her aim.

'Good work, Bertha,' cried Millicent. 'Now we'll nip back home and come back tomorrow and see the results.'

But Bertha had spotted a lone mouse scuttling through the grass and pounced, grabbing the struggling rodent by the throat and quickly killing it.

'Ah, a light supper,' she exclaimed. 'Just the ticket after a good pee.'

Millicent was forced to stand by while Bertha slowly gummed her way through the snack. Suddenly, Millicent became aware of a radio signal coming in through the speaker imbedded in her extra microchip. That's strange, she thought, Tom hasn't been able to get through because of the high mountains and deep valleys blocking the reception. I wonder how he managed it.

She tuned into the frequency and heard a familiar voice. 'Are you receiving me?'

It was King!

'Receiving,' replied Millicent. 'King, is that you?'

'Sure is, Princess.'

'But how did you get my frequency and call sign?'

There was a chuckle from the speaker. 'You forget, the FBI haf vays und means ov breaking into any frequency,' he replied in an awful German accent.

'Well, what do you want?' Millicent replied, somewhat annoyed that her channel had been compromised.

'Listen, Princess,' King replied with amusement, 'I've managed to dig up some information on the cocaine issue. I've got an address for the owner of the two Rottweilers' property; thought you might be interested in co-operating with the investigation.'

Millicent immediately became interested, and was secretly flattered and surprised that King would share the information with her.

'I could be,' she replied nonchalantly 'if you feel you really need the help.'

'Well,' King chuckled, 'as they say, eight paws are better than four. And besides, you might pick up a few clues on how a real investigator operates.'

She ignored the barb and listened while he gave her the address and his plan of attack. But at that moment, a ferocious dog bark from close by startled them and Bertha got such a shock she managed to squirt an extra cannabis plant for good measure. Millicent quickly signed off agreeing to meet him at the assigned location and she and Bertha took off with the hounds from hell on their heels.

Millicent was amazed at the sudden agility of Bertha as they sprinted back towards the farmhouse. She was quite skittish, even to suddenly leaping in the air over tree stumps and other obstacles and giggling as she hit the ground running. Millicent had trouble keeping up with her and was forced to increase her speed.

They arrived back home far outstripping the dogs who gave up the chase at the boundary. They flopped down on the back verandah with Bertha uncharacteristically rolling on her back, purring and laughing with her paws clutching at the air like a frisky kitten. Then she suddenly jumped up and swiped at a spider scuttling along the railing.

Suddenly it all became clear. 'Bertha,' Millicent mewed reproachfully, 'You're stoned!'

'What?' giggled Bertha. 'Don't be stupid, I never touch the stuff.'

'That mouse you caught over there, it was probably full of dope! I saw where they'd been nibbling the packets of dope when I was over there before. They're probably full of the stuff. You may not realise it but you've just had your first sample of hash-mouse cookies.'

Bertha suddenly became very serious. 'Well, come to think of it, I'm not feeling any pain. Maybe that stuff isn't so bad after all.'

'Well, don't get used to it, baby, you could become addicted and you could be in for a downer when it wears off.'

Millicent met King at the appointed time and location. It was night-time, of course and Millicent had been forced to escape just after dinner to reach the designated address in time. Pat and Jenny had become quite used to her disappearing for hours at a time; sometimes she'd be gone all night, returning exhausted early in the morning for breakfast.

She met up with King at the entrance to a property just outside of town. High iron gates with a heavy security chain protected the entrance but it was simple enough for the two slim cats to slip through the bars and, creeping and darting from cover to cover, they made their way down a long gravel pathway. The house was set well back from the main road and when it eventually came into view, Millicent stopped and stared.

This was no ordinary house; it was huge, almost a mansion; double storey with tall white columns reaching from the front portico to the gabled, terracotta tiled roof. Several lights shone through the panelled, colonial-style windows on the ground floor, and from a giant brick chimney, a ribbon of grey smoke drifted in the still night air. A wide driveway led off to the right servicing a triple-sized garage. The front garden looked to be beautifully landscaped with trimmed green lawn and tall hedges forming concentric circles around a central, white marble, Victorian-era fountain that splashed, gurgled and shone in the moonlight.

'Wow, this is serious money,' exclaimed Millicent. 'More North Shore or Toorak.'

'There's not another one of this calibre in the area,' replied King. 'It hardly fits into the alternative style of living, does it?

'Well, it's certainly alternative to where I'm living,' replied Millicent.

'And it's so remote and off the beaten track,' King mused. 'Why would that be I wonder?'

'Maybe they want to get away from it all, without getting too far away from it,' she said. 'And you say this belongs to the elusive Mr Delmonte?' Millicent queried.

'Hmm, supposedly,' purred King, thoughtfully. 'Let's take a look around.'

They explored the front garden and found nothing suspicious and then moved around to the back. Again there was no evidence of anything amiss so King suggested they try to gain entrance to the palatial home and check it out.

'What do you suggest?' Millicent whispered.

'Let's look for an open window, someone may have got careless,' he whispered back.

'I noticed a vine trellis attached to the side wall,' said Millicent. 'I might be able to get up there and check the second-floor windows.'

'Right,' King replied. 'I'll check out the ground floor. But be careful, I don't want you falling and breaking your neck.'

'I always land on my feet – in *any* circumstance,' she replied, sanguinely.

They went their separate ways and King headed for one of the lit front windows near the chimney to see if he could look in. The drapes were drawn but there was a chink where the drapes met that allowed him a limited view. He heard male voices talking but could only see the back of the head of one of the speakers above the back of a wing chair drawn up next to the open fire place. From his secret pouch he produced a small listening device which he placed against the window and put his ear to it.

'Well, you've made your position quite clear.' The growl coming from the wing chair was harsh and abrupt. 'I'm appalled and insulted that you should even suggest such a thing. However, I will think about everything you've said and get back to you when I've made my decision. But I warn you, I will not be blackmailed and I will not tolerate interference in my business dealings.'

'Of course, I have no actual proof, as you say,' came the reply, 'but I thought it best to warn you that suspicions are rife. I just thought a change of location might be, shall we say, healthier for you. I hear Darwin is nice at this time of the year.'

'It's the wet season, you fool,' retorted the other man.

'I'm sure this gentleman's information is completely ungrounded, Dad,' a sweet, cultured female voice cut in, 'but you know how people gossip in these small towns. And I'm also sure time and further investigation will allay any of his suspicions. Now I think it best that you leave. I'll see you out.'

King recognised the voice of the gentleman caller but before he could fathom the implications, there was a crash from the side of the house where Millicent had headed; the front garden suddenly became emblazoned with security lights and, worst of all, the vicious barking of guard dogs filled the air and made the fur rise on his back. He immediately flew for the nearest tree, an Acacia, scaled the trunk and leapt into the comparative safety of its branches and foliage. The front door burst open and a man appeared holding a shotgun at the ready.

King was aware of a streak of fur flashing past in the direction of the front gate closely pursued by the barking Rottweilers. He called out to her but she had disappeared. The sound of his call immediately brought the Rottweilers to a sudden screeching halt, their paws throwing up a shower of gravel. Thinking their prey had somehow shot up the tree they continued barking furiously as they approached the trunk and looked up. Oops, King thought, as he climbed higher into the branches and looked down. This could be a stand-off for quite some time. At least it will give Milly a chance to escape.

But then he noticed the man in the doorway lift the shotgun to his shoulder and take aim vaguely in his direction. King quickly skipped behind the trunk of the tree just as the man fired. There was an enormous explosion and the pellets ripped into the foliage and tiny branches sending them scattering in all directions. King clung on to the trunk, instinctively ducking.

'Bloody possums!' he heard the man mutter as he reloaded the weapon and approached the tree. King cautiously crept further around the tree trunk keeping it between him and the hunter.

'Wait! Bruce! Don't fire!' The authoritative cry came from the young woman who had followed the man through the front door accompanied by the visitor she was escorting out.

Bruce hesitated and turned to her. 'It's just a bloody possum.'

'No it's not, it's a cat, you fool. I can see him from here.'

'What's the difference?' the man with the gun responded, 'It'll still give Randy and Rodney a tasty supper.'

'Put the gun down,' the woman ordered, 'and get a ladder. And for God's sake take those two vicious mongrels with you and chain them up.'

The man grumbled but grabbed the dogs by their collars and dragged them off.

The young woman and her visitor approached the tree making soothing sounds to calm King. King crept cautiously out onto a branch and looked down. I was right, he thought, recognising the visitor. It's Dr Fellini. I hope he doesn't give me away.

Bruce returned with a long extension ladder and leaned it up against the tree.

'Now, I want you to climb up there and bring him down,' the young woman said, 'and don't hurt him.'

'Maybe it would be better if I climbed up and got him,' interjected Dr Fellini. 'After all I have had more experience with cats than Bruce.'

'Oh, thank you, Dr Fellini,' said the young woman gratefully.

King suddenly recognised her as the young 'man' he and Millicent had seen at the cocaine factory! Mind you, she was looking quite different and ladylike now, dressed in a long, flowing, purple caftan with her hair piled up on top of her head and caught by a diamond clasp. Ah, he thought, we're certainly on the right track. She called the other man in the wing back chair, *Dad*! So this is the infamous Mr Delmonte's daughter! It's a family business!

Dr Fellini climbed the ladder and softly called King's name. King peeked out from behind the tree trunk and mewed. Fellini gestured to him and King responded by carefully negotiating the branches and climbing down to within Fellini's reach. The vet gently picked him up, cradled him in his arm and bent his head to King's ear. 'What are you doing out here, my friend?' he whispered. 'A little investigative work of your own?'

King purred and nodded.

'Well, we'll see if I can help if you're willing to take the chance.'

King nodded again and Dr Fellini began to retreat backwards down the ladder whispering, 'Play the exhausted, injured cat. I'll try and leave you here overnight so you can look the place over for the evidence we need.'

Dr Fellini arrived back on the ground and handed King to the young woman. King lay in her arms, mewing pathetically and looking at her with his captivating golden eyes. 'I think he's a bit injured. He's a beautiful and very expensive cat – a Burmese. His name is King. I know his owners so would you mind keeping him safe tonight and I'll get them to pick him up tomorrow morning? It would be a bit late calling them now.'

'Why of course,' said the young woman. 'I'll get a box and rug to keep him warm and he can sleep in my room. I wouldn't dare let him out of the house with those two Rottweiler brutes running around.'

Well, thank God for that, King thought, relieved.

'That's very kind of you, Amethyst,' Dr Fellini smiled.

Amethyst, King thought. So her name is Amethyst. Well, she's certainly as beautiful as one but it's still a bit of an alternative name.'

'Please call me Amy, Dr Fellini,' she requested with a demure smile. 'I hate being called Amethyst, it sounds so pretentious.'

I wonder what *Millicent* will think of that remark when I tell her, smiled King to himself.

Dr Fellini bade her goodnight and headed back down the drive. Amy cuddled King firmly and made her way back into the house, talking to him soothingly. The security lights were doused and night once again enveloped the mansion. Randy and Rodney were unchained and returned to patrolling their domain.

Millicent, hidden in the darkness outside the security gates behind a shrub, watched Dr Fellini walk down the driveway. A cane toad silently hopped up behind her and spat. She jumped, causing her to land almost at Dr Fellini's feet. He stopped and looked down at her.

'Well, well, well, if it isn't Millicent. And what are you doing out here, little lady? You wouldn't be assisting your friend King, would you? Or do you have other business out here? I think it best that we leave him by himself to get on with his work, eh?'

She was about to make a run for it when he scooped her up and walked with her to his car hidden nearby under a drooping tree, opened the passenger door and threw her in.

'You're a long way from home, my girl, and in a very dangerous area. I'll give you a lift back to the farmhouse.'

Millicent was furious with his interference but had no alternative but to comply.

When they arrived back at the farmhouse, Dr Fellini opened the passenger side door and released her.

Thanks a lot! she fumed, as she jumped down and made her way around to the back verandah. I can't even get in touch with King on my radio; he didn't give me his call sign or frequency. Bloody incompetent FBI!

She had a mental image of King being torn to pieces by the vicious Rottweilers and a shiver ran through her body.

'Hi, sweetie,' came Bertha's voice from the cat box in the corner. 'Out carousing again, you little trollop?'

Bertha's voice was slow and sleepy. Oh Lord, sighed Millicent. Bertha's been hitting the hash-mouse cookies again. She'd have to give her a good talking to in the morning. It was a waste of time now as Bertha was completely spaced out. Millicent settled down on a cane armchair, her mind replaying the events of the evening.

Several hours later, she was awoken by a radio signal being transmitted to her.

'King?' she quickly transmitted back. 'Is that you?'

'Sure is, Princess. Thought I'd let you know I'm still in the land of the living. I'm installed in the lovely Amethyst's bedroom – on her bed as a matter of fact, and *very* comfortable.'

'Who is Amethyst?' asked Millicent with just a hint of jealousy in her voice.

'Old man Delmonte's daughter,' he replied with a satisfied smile. 'I think she's the one we saw at the cocaine property the other night, only she was dressed as a man. Actually she prefers to be called by the shortened version of her name, Amy. She thinks it's less pretentious.'

Millicent ignored the sarcastic implication. 'What's happening out there? How did you get away from those dreadful dogs? And why are you sharing the *delightful* Amethyst's bed?'

'Whoa, Princess, I'll tell you all about it when I see you. In the meantime I've been exploring the house while Amy's sleeping. There are art works worth millions and I found a safe in the floor next to the fireplace. I wasn't able to crack it though. I've been through the desk and filing cabinet. That was a bit tricky. Lucky I had my lock picks in my pouch. I found quite a few copies of Sydney newspaper articles about high-ranking police and politicians suspected of corruption but no direct mention of Delmonte being involved in the drug trade. Apart from that, I've found nothing to implicate Delmonte or any link to the cocaine or cannabis. I can't even find copies of deeds to that property we visited. If they exist, they're probably in the safe. I'm at the computer as we speak but so far I haven't been able to crack the password. I'll keep in touch, should be back home tomorrow. Sleep tight.' With that he cut the transmission.

'But wait! – King?' But he was gone. Well, at least he's safe for the time being, she thought. She curled up on the chair and dozed off, at least a little reassured.

Chapter 11

King again attempted to break the password for the computer. *'Randy'*, he typed in – *'Access denied'* came the prompt. *'Rodney, Rottweiler, Amy and Amethyst'* he also tried but to no avail. It could be any of a million words, he thought. He really needed a good hacker but where could he find one? Suddenly an idea hit him. His partner! Dr Fellini! He's a trained FBI agent – he could probably get in; but how to get him access to the computer while the Delmontes were out of the way? He'd have to work on that one.

He was suddenly surprised by Bruce who was doing his nightly security rounds. He quickly slipped off the keyboard and slunk behind the couch but it was too late. Bruce, who was obviously not a cat lover, spied him and gave chase. King tore out of the office, his paws slipping on the marble tiles, closely followed by Bruce. King pelted through the ground floor, trapped at every avenue. The windows were all shut and he could find no means of escape. He managed to knock over several *objets d'art*, which forced Bruce to curse and try to save them before they could crash to the floor. In desperation, King squawked and flung himself at the front door, the impact causing an immediate bowel movement, which stank like the devil and ran down the door. He then hid behind the umbrella stand that held the frightening shotgun, awaiting his fate. Bruce was hit by the sudden stench, exclaimed his disgust loudly and automatically opened the door for the smell to escape. King grabbed the chance and shot out.

Randy and Rodney, the Rottweilers, alarmed by the commotion, were waiting. The brutal barking erupted once again and they dived for him. With the speed and agility of a panther King threw himself at Randy, spitting and screaming as he sank his claws into the dog's nose. Randy yelped and shook his head violently. King timed the thrust beautifully and at the apex of the headshake retracted his claws and flew through the air over the head of Rodney who snapped viciously but missed. The force of Randy's headshake propelled King several metres away, giving him the advantage of distance between him and his foes. He hit the ground on the run and shot off with the speed of a gazelle in flight from a ravenous lioness. The Rottweilers gave chase but King had the advantage of speed and intricate swerves and soon outdistanced them. A gunshot rang out, no doubt from the hands of Bruce, followed by a blaze of security lights and lights from the bedrooms but it was too late. King had already reached the front gates, slipped through the bars effortlessly and was off.

He headed straight back to the surgery, slipped through his personal cat flap, hit the computer and wrote his report to his partner, Dr Fellini, who would read it in the morning.

Millicent awoke to find Bertha studying her intently.

'Good morning,' Millicent said, 'and how are we feeling this morning?'

'I'm fine,' said Bertha, 'slept like a log.'

She did a little turn and settled back in the same spot facing Millicent.

'Where were you last night?' she asked.

Millicent wondered just how much information it was safe to relate to Bertha but decided it was time to trust her.

'I was out checking on the Delmonte property.'

'And why would you be doing that? I hear they have guard dogs on the prowl.'

'Yes, they have – Rottweilers, as you said,' Millicent informed her, remembering only too well the danger she had put herself in. 'I had to take the risk.' She relented and told Bertha about her suspicions regarding the cocaine trade but omitted any mention of her secret identity.

Bertha sat thinking for quite some time before she replied. 'They're relatively new to the area – *nouveau riche*, as Pat calls them. They keep to themselves apparently. As far as I can tell, nobody has actually laid eyes on old man Delmonte himself. It's rumoured he has a few rough-looking staff that look after him and the property. He's also supposed to have a rather beautiful daughter but I've never seen her.' She paused thoughtfully. 'Cocaine – well, the town can certainly do without that. They tolerate the bit of hash around the place and I must admit I can see the reason why – it seems to have done wonders for my aches and pains – but hard stuff is certainly frowned upon. I wonder if Pat and Jenny know. They'd be out there with flame throwers in a flash. So would most of the town, I suspect. Not a good image for the town.'

'But Nimbin has a reputation for drug tolerance,' Millicent said.

'Mostly overstated by the media,' Bertha replied contemptuously. 'No, this is a lovely peaceful town and most of the community are friendly tolerant folk. They just want the simple life free of too much political or commercial interference.'

'Would you be in favour of helping me to root out the undesirables?' Millicent asked tentatively.

'Well, of course,' replied Bertha. 'Not that I'd be much use with my arthritis and neuralgia and sinus and acid kidneys and asthma and …'

'I didn't know you were asthmatic,' Millicent said, not entirely surprised, considering Bertha was a bit of a hypochondriac.

'Oh, yes, since I was a kitten,' Bertha moaned dramatically. 'Haven't you heard me wheezing all the time?'

'Well, yes,' replied Millicent, 'but I thought you were just purring.'

'I try not to complain,' said Bertha stoically.

'Speaking of your acid kidney complaint,' said Millicent, trying to change the subject away from Bertha's plethora of ageing symptoms, 'have you checked the cannabis plants next door?'

Rather smugly, Bertha actually smiled, and rose to her feet. 'Come with me and we'll have a look.' She led Millicent across the lawn and through the fence into the next property. Being broad daylight, Millicent was continuously on the lookout for the mongrels but to her surprise they were nowhere to be seen.

They slipped through the chicken-wire fence and made their way to the spot where Bertha had performed her acidic ablutions. Millicent was as amazed as any scientist would be on discovering the cure for cancer. Sure enough, the plants targeted by Bertha had definitely wilted; their leaves and flowers that were just beginning to form, hung like sad green streamers the night after a party, and some of the lower shoots were actually curling and turning brown!

'Bertha, that is *amazing*!' exclaimed Millicent. 'I can't believe it would work so quickly.' She sniffed the plant and quickly recoiled from the strong acidic stench that still permeated the plant and the soil in which it had been planted.

Bertha smiled in great satisfaction and in celebration lifted her tail and shot out another lethal squirt at a nearby plant.

'You've got to admit, it's a powerful pee,' she smiled in pride.

'Yes indeed,' agreed Millicent, 'but I wonder if it would work on a coca plantation.'

'Oh, I don't know if I could manage a whole plantation,' replied Bertha, hesitantly. 'I might need a bit of help and a whole lot of water nearby.'

'It's still a thought,' said Millicent, her mind spinning with possibilities.

'Why are you so suddenly interested in ridding the area of drugs?' asked Bertha suspiciously.

Millicent thought for a moment and then decided to take Bertha into her full confidence. After all, if she went around blurting it out nobody would take any notice of her, suspecting Bertha now had Alzheimer's to add to her list of complaints. 'Bertha, this is strictly confidential and nobody is to know, agreed?'

'Agreed,' Bertha repeated breathlessly.

'It's a Government priority.' Millicent looked around to make sure they weren't being overheard. 'I'm actually a member of C.I.A.D.E.D.'

'Well, you don't have to spell it out for me, Millicent,' Bertha said rather archly. 'I'm not exactly senile yet.'

There was a pause before Bertha whispered, 'What's a ciaded?'

'C.I.A.D.E.D.,' Millicent enunciated slowly. 'Cat's Investigation Agency Drug Enforcement Division. Highly secretive.'

Bertha clutched her breast and gave an involuntary squirt, completely un-aimed, and hit a ripe tomato on a nearby vine. 'Oh my God, you're a spy?'

'I'm actually an agent,' Millicent replied, with just a hint of pride.

'A secret agent?' Bertha squeaked in excitement.

'Shhhhh,' Millicent hissed attempting to quieten her with a paw over her mouth. 'Keep your voice down!'

'Ooh, sorry,' apologised Bertha, whispering. 'But you're a real spy, I mean a secret agent?'

Millicent nodded and waited for the shock to subside.

'Well, I'll be ...' Bertha gaped, very impressed. 'So you aren't a stray from Blue Knob, you're from ... the Federal Government?'

Millicent nodded sagely.

'I knew there was something different about you,' said Bertha. 'I just thought you were an uppity show cat with an attitude.'

Millicent's justification and explanation was suddenly interrupted by a radio message coming in. It was King in a highly agitated frame of mind. He almost yelled through her inner speaker, causing her to wince painfully.

'Millicent, we've got big trouble! You've got to get over here to the surgery as quickly as you can! – It's Dr Fellini! – He's dead! I think he's been murdered!'

Hardly believing her ears, Millicent stared at Bertha in shock.

Chapter 12

As luck would have it, Pat and Jenny were about to leave to visit the market and Millicent jumped up onto Pat's backpack, which was lying on the floor, and took up her usual position. She tilted her head up to Pat and mewed pathetically.

'Oh, will you look at that, Jen,' Pat laughed delightedly. 'Milly knows we're going into town and she wants to come with us.'

'She's such a smart cat,' Jenny said, lovingly stroking Millicent's head, 'aren't you, Milly?'

Millicent managed to ignore the abbreviation of her name and mewed and purred even louder for sympathetic effect.

'Oh, alright, girl,' laughed Pat, picking up the backpack with Millicent firmly attached, 'you're not really subtle, are you?'

Subtlety I can't always afford, mewed Millicent to herself, as she was hefted into position.

Pat and Jenny were lucky to get a parking spot in Sibley Street just across the park from the veterinary surgery. There was a police car outside the surgery and two uniformed policemen standing outside on guard. The entrance was roped off and a few people stood around chatting excitedly in whispered conversation, occasionally pointing to the surgery and nodding.

'A bit of excitement outside the vet's,' Pat announced to Jenny. 'Wonder what's going on?'

'There's old Jack with his pet goat,' said Jenny, indicating the old man standing on the footpath with the kid on a tether.

He was talking to another policeman who was writing notes in his notebook.

'Maybe there's been a break-in,' said Jenny. 'Someone after drugs, I suppose.'

'Let's wander over and have a squiz,' Pat said, as she opened the car door.

Before Pat could get out Millicent jumped off Jenny's shoulder and bolted out onto the road and took off across the park.

'Millicent, come back!' yelled a distraught Jenny. 'Watch the traffic! – Millicent!'

But Millicent ignored the plea and tore across Cullen Street. Luckily traffic was light and she made it across safely.

'What the hell's got into her?' exclaimed Pat, with a sigh of relief.

'God knows,' Jenny replied. 'She must think we're taking her to the vet's again.'

'Smartarse cat,' Pat replied. 'Bring the harness and lead from the glovebox,' she called as she checked for oncoming traffic and quickly followed. 'We can't have her running around loose'.

Millicent darted down the short lane between the legs of the onlookers and immediately saw King sitting on a window ledge opposite the entrance to the surgery. Seeing her, he jumped down and headed around the corner. She followed, leaving a short distance between them and the onlookers for privacy.

'What happened?' Millicent cried in concern as they hid behind a packing case left at the rear of the building.

'Fellini's dead!' King whispered in shock. 'I came in this morning to see if he'd read my report and found him lying on the examination table! I thought he was asleep. But when I jumped up onto his chest to wake him, there was no reaction. I jumped up and down on him like I usually have to do when he's asleep and I want my breakfast, but there was no reaction. I checked his heartbeat and there wasn't one. He was dead.'

'But how?' Millicent asked in astonishment.

'I don't know!' replied King, fiercely at a loss. 'He was in the best of health when I saw him last night at the Delmontes'.'

'And he was fine when he dropped me off home,' Millicent replied, puzzled. 'Did you see him after that?'

'No, I was out on a bit of – reconnaissance. I didn't get in until this morning.'

Millicent could only guess at the kind of reconnaissance he was out on.

'The buzz outside the surgery is that he committed suicide,' King said in disbelief. 'But that can't be true – he had no reason to commit suicide. FBI agents don't commit suicide unless they are trapped in an impossible situation and they face torture or certain death. His cover wasn't blown or in jeopardy – everybody thought he was just a local vet.'

King was obviously still in shock so Millicent was forced to prod him for further information. 'So you actually saw the body?'

'Of course, I told you, I jumped on his chest and felt for a heartbeat! I went outside to see if I could inveigle anybody in to find him and get help and then Waratah, the receptionist, and the old bloke with the goat arrived, saw the door open, came in, found him and raised the alarm.'

'Describe the scene to me, as you remember it. Were there any obvious wounds?'

King took a deep breath and recalled the incident in full as he had been trained. 'No. He was lying on the examination table.' He paused tactfully before he continued. 'He wasn't wearing any clothes.'

'What?' Millicent cried in amazement. 'Why not? I mean, it was pretty cold last night. And that examination table is made of stainless steel. He must've been freezing – do you think maybe he froze to death?'

'No, it was definitely his heart,' King assured her. 'There were no wounds. His clothes were just dumped on the chair like they usually are before he goes to bed.'

'But surely he doesn't go to bed on the examination table?' Millicent asked incredulously.

'No, of course not,' King replied, admonishingly. 'He has an apartment above the surgery. He sleeps upstairs.'

'Then why was he naked in the surgery?' Millicent asked, puzzled.

'Well, maybe he got undressed ready to go up to bed, felt a bit woozy, and sat or lay on the table to recover and had a heart attack,' King replied uneasily, obviously leaving some detail unspoken.

Millicent picked up on his evasiveness and asked, 'What else, King? You're leaving something out.'

King looked uncomfortable and eventually capitulated. 'Alright. He sometimes *entertained* young women in the surgery. There was an empty syringe on the floor. He had a ... habit. He wasn't hooked,' he added quickly.

'He overdosed?' Millicent asked incredulously.

'No!' King almost shouted. 'He was a pro, he knew the dangers. He wasn't a stupid junkie. He was just a bit ... kinky.'

'Kinky?' Millicent repeated in amazement.

'Well, he sort of got turned on by the cold stainless steel table top,' King responded unwillingly.

'So,' Millicent continued, ignoring the obvious sexual connotations, 'just how many young women did he *entertain* on the stainless steel examination table in the surgery?'

'Not many ... well, a few,' he admitted reluctantly. 'There was a girl called Freesia, worked part time at the bakery, Poppy from the craft shop, Lily from the library, and a glass blower – I never got her name.'

'It was probably Pansy, if he was still following the floral influence,' Millicent replied sardonically. 'Well, he certainly had a bunch of them, didn't he? – or should that be a bouquet?'

'There was something else I've just remembered.' King paused, recalling. 'A perfume – sort of musky – not sweet, but – different.'

'Probably left over from one of his floral tributes,' Millicent said dismissively.

'He's dead!' King responded heatedly. 'And he was my partner. I think a little more respect and a little less levity are in order.'

Millicent stretched and licked her back. 'Well, he was surely *active* in the community.' She had almost dismissed the demise of the vet as being an overdose when she remembered King's remark when he radioed her. 'You said he'd been murdered. Why did you jump to that conclusion?'

'The pharmacy up the road was broken into last night, as well. There was nothing significant stolen. They're very careful about locking all the harmful drugs in a strongroom every night. So, if they failed at the pharmacy, wouldn't you think they may have a go at the vet's surgery?'

'Possibly,' Millicent conceded. 'But surely Dr Fellini kept his drugs under lock and key as well?'

'Yes, he did, but if they were a new gang in town, they mightn't know that. It could be worth a try.' King was now in full swing in his argument. 'Maybe they broke into the surgery not expecting Dr Fellini to be in there; he attacked them, or tried to defend himself, they hit him over the head and he had a heart attack.'

'But why would they strip him? He obviously wasn't tortured. You said there were no obvious signs of physical attack. Surely you would have noticed a lump or a wound on his head. Was the front door or window forced?'

'No. Whoever got in must've come through the front door.'

'Then Fellini must have known them and let them in,' she concluded.

King scratched his ear, furiously. 'It looks like it.' Another thought struck him. 'It was cold you said, right?'

'Yes,' she replied.

'Well, the electric heater was turned off! He always left the heater on when he worked – or, er, played – at night. So whoever was with him, murderer or not, must've turned the heater off when they switched the lights out. One switch is above the other.'

'Did you have the chance to tell what had been in the syringe?

'No, we'll have to wait for the autopsy. They've taken the body to the local hospital. I've got an informer there. She'll find out and let me know.'

'She'll?' Millicent repeated a little archly. 'How many women *informers* do you have on your books? And are you also partial to entertaining them on the stainless steel examination table?'

'What can I say, Princess?' he said with the confidence of his masculinity. 'I'm a fully operational tom. I have to use all of my talents.'

'Both you and Dr Fellini, by the sound of it,' she haughtily conceded.

'We're males, for God's sake, we have … appetites.'

Millicent recalled that King had been neutered so he was obviously bragging the way toms do to protect their masculinity. She was saved from any retort by Pat's voice calling loudly, 'Milly? … Milly? … Where are you?'

'*Millicent*, for God's sake!' She turned to King. 'I'll be in touch.' And with that, she turned, flicked her tail in dismissal and sauntered back down the alley.

'I'll have to report this to headquarters,' he called after her.

'We'll both have to,' she called back to him.

On the way home in the ute, Pat and Jenny were upset and mystified by the death of the kind Dr Fellini.

'Carl, from the greengrocers,' said Jenny, 'reckoned there was a gang of bikies he hadn't seen before, that rode into town yesterday. I wonder if they had anything to do with the break-ins or poor Dr Fellini's death?'

'Oh, the bikies always get the blame,' replied Pat in their defence. 'Lucrezia Borgia was an aristocrat and I'll bet she never threw her leg over a Harley. No, I reckon it was suicide,' Pat continued confidently. 'Veterinarians have the highest rate of suicides of any of the professions.'

'Do they?' replied Jenny in astonishment. 'I thought it was dentists.'

'No, that's an old wives' tale,' smirked Pat knowingly. 'Statistically, white males in any medical profession are high on the list, as are white female painters and sculptors, by the way. Surprising we don't have a lot more suicides out here in the artistic colony. Especially with some of the work I've seen around the place. Some of them definitely aren't well.'

Bertha was positively agog while Millicent relayed the details of the morning's events.

'Break-ins, suicide or possible murder?' Bertha exclaimed in excitement. 'This is the biggest thing that's happened in Nimbin since the Aquarius Festival! The town will go into shock. Reefers will be lighting up the sky like fireworks!'

'I somehow tend to agree with King – I have a strong suspicion Fellini was murdered.'

'What makes you think that?' asked Bertha breathlessly, whether from shock or asthma Millicent couldn't tell.

'Instinct,' replied Millicent, 'and Fellini was out at the Delmonte place last night, according to King, and he overheard them having a bit of a row.'

'What about?'

'King couldn't say; or wouldn't say. He claims he didn't hear enough but strong words were exchanged apparently, and threats were made, and a few hours later Dr Fellini turns up dead in suspicious circumstances.' Before she could continue to postulate any further, King was back on the radio. She moved away and crawled under the back stairs for privacy.

'What is it, King?'

'I'm going to get Delmonte. I know he's tied up in the drug trade and I know he's responsible for Fellini's death!' He sounded very angry and appeared to have lost his usual cool, suave attitude.

'But listen, King, we aren't even certain yet that it was murder. We need more evidence. As yet we have no actual proof of Delmonte's involvement. You couldn't find anything incriminating last night. I agree he's suspicious and we have to follow the lead through but we have to be careful and wait until we're more sure of the facts.'

'I just got the report from my snitch at the hospital. According to forensics, Fellini was poisoned with a heavy dose of Pentobarbital. You know what that is?' Before she could answer he continued harshly, 'It's the drug they use to euthanise animals. It sends them off to sleep and the victim slips into cardiac arrest.'

'Could that have been the perfume you smelled?' she asked.

'No,' he replied with certainty. 'Pentobarbital has a very distinctive odour. God knows I've smelled it often enough at the surgery.' He pondered for a moment. 'Mind you, the perfume I smelled could have been used to disguise the Pentobarbital – like a room deodoriser.'

'But if it was suicide, wouldn't that be the likely drug he'd use?'

'He'd hardly inject himself and then spray the room with deodorant, would he? He didn't kill himself!' he said forcefully. 'He had too much to live for. We were on the verge of uncovering this cocaine business. I'm sure that property belongs to Delmonte but I can't get at the deeds. Even if it's not his name on the titles, he's the boss of the outfit, I know!'

'Let's just wait until I do some further checking,' Millicent remonstrated. 'I'm waiting to get word back from the Agency. My superior is sending me mug shots of the men suspected of involvement in the drug trade that can't be accounted for. As soon as they arrive I'll contact you and you can take a look. This Delmonte person would have to be identified and no one seems to know for sure what he looks like.'

'Well, it's not what you'd call a common name,' replied King. There was a pause and then he asked, 'You haven't mentioned my name in your reports, have you?'

'No, of course not, why would I?' Millicent lied. 'I didn't want to compromise your position. And likewise, I hope you haven't mentioned me or my assignment?'

'No, you're still in the clear,' was King's reply.

'So don't you think we should wait for further instructions from our chiefs before you go ahead with any direct action?'

'I want revenge now,' King stated coldly.

Millicent hesitated before replying, thinking King must really be upset to intend hobbling Delmonte without sufficient proof. They'd all lost partners in operations before – her mind flew back to Kitty in New Zealand – it went with the job. They knew the risks and they took them. 'Listen, King, I'm working on an idea to flush them out into the open and destroy their crops so just hold tight until I get back to you with my plan, alright?'

There was another long pause before King replied. 'Okay,' he finally conceded, 'but it better be soon. I have personal reasons to take that murdering rat out.'

Millicent signed off with, 'Hold tight, King, I'll be back in touch. What's your radio call sign and wavelength?'

'I'll get back to you. I might be out of range.'

He cut off contact. Millicent hoped he wouldn't go ahead on his own without contacting her. She quickly returned to the back verandah and approached Bertha. 'Bertha, you told me there were quite a few other cats who had your acid urine condition. Do you have a list of them or any way to contact them?'

'Oh, yes,' replied Bertha, 'we have a meeting every month. It's a sort of social club. We call ourselves the Pee-hew Club. We all get together and have a few laughs and a bit of low acid supper. I might drag along a few of those delicious mice from next door. That should give the night a bit of a lift.'

'When's the next meeting?' Millicent asked.

Bertha took her time to remember but finally came up with, 'The night after tomorrow, why?'

'Would it be possible for me to attend – as a guest, of course? I have a little proposition I want to put to them.'

'Oh, I'm sure that would be alright. Actually, I'd like you to meet them, they're a fun group. And with my supper offering, they'll be even funnier.'

Chapter 13

The appointed evening arrived but not before Millicent had had the chance to exchange emails with Tom in Canberra. The exchange proved quite interesting but had little that was of use to her and the promised mug shots weren't attached. She was asked to maintain vigilance and forward any clues she could uncover. She again requested the mug shots and any other information she could use. This assignment was turning into a nightmare. She absorbed all the information and stored it on her recording chip.

The venue was in an old flower nursery shed just outside of town and Bertha had been busy storing and preparing her supper for the occasion. She had carefully laid out the mice they had caught at Binthere-Dunthat to dry in the sun, which turned them into lovely crunchy cookies. However, she'd obviously given in to temptation and sampled some of her offerings as she was quite lively and frisky. This did not go unnoticed by Pat and Jenny who suspected that poor old Bertha was coming to the end of the line and turning senile.

Millicent located her backpack which she'd stored under the house and packed the supper. Together they dragged the bulging bag to the nursery shed. Millicent was amazed at the number of cats assembled and the security measures they had in place in case they were interrupted by the mongrel dogs of the area.

On arrival they were greeted with much wailing and jumping on, and rolling about, by the lively members. But Millicent's eye was taken by a most attractive ginger tom that sat to the side of the celebrations, watching but not joining in the festivities.

'Who is that?' Millicent hissed to Bertha, eyeing the handsome stranger.

'That, my dear, is the lovely Marcel. He's only new to the area apparently, but quite a hit with the ladies, I hear. Personally I don't go for redheads, particularly the shorthaired domestic variety. Nothing personal, dear, but I do think cats should have lovely long fluffy hair.'

'But he's got the most gorgeous green eyes,' Millicent said admiringly. 'Where is he living?'

'Don't know exactly, he just turned up a few days ago.'

To her surprise, Marcel stood up, stretched sensually and slowly made his way towards them. Normally she would have immediately gone into her *dori* defence stance but there was something unthreatening about Marcel which gave her a feeling that he meant her no harm. He purred and gently rubbed himself against her. A shiver of excitement ran through her body, or maybe it was static electricity. Before a formal introduction could take place, Bertha's voice rose above the surrounding caterwauling. She was standing on the seat of a red tractor, her front paws stretched out commanding attention.

'Friends,' she announced, 'we have a guest speaker with us tonight who has graciously offered to address us on a very important topic. I ask that you give her a warm welcome and your full attention.' She paused for effect and stretched out a front leg in Millicent's direction. 'Fellow felines, may I present the Oriental Shorthair and Gold Medal winner of her breed in many prestigious competitions – the lovely Ms Millicent!'

The gathering roared its approval and, somewhat embarrassed, Millicent smiled at Marcel and made her way to the podium.

Leaping nimbly onto the tractor seat she paused, waiting for the assembly to quieten down. Dozens of shining cats' eyes gleamed at her through the soft moonlit venue. Suddenly, seemingly on cue, the moon cleared a cloud and like a spotlight, a silver moonbeam shone through a hole in the ancient timber roof creating a silver halo around her, and the gathering suddenly hushed at the sight.

'Bertha, and fellow furry friends,' she began, 'thank you so much for your warm welcome. Although I am only a newcomer to your delightful town, I have been made to feel quite at home here already. Your beautiful locality is a constant joy and the alternative lifestyle you have adopted imbues the place with a peace and tranquillity that must be protected at all costs.' There was a chorus of agreement and she paused to let her words register. 'That is why I have come to speak to you all this evening. Upon my travels and exploration of the town and its environs, it has come to my attention that all is not as it appears.'

There was a hush in the congregation as Millicent's words questioned their idyllic way of life and sent a shiver of query and consternation in the minds of the listeners.

'We are all aware that some of the inhabitants of the district practise the cultivation of small quantities of marijuana for personal use. Now, although most of us consider this harmless, it is nonetheless unlawful in the eyes of the constabulary and in most cases a blind eye is turned to the practice.'

'And rightly so,' came a cat-call from a particularly hippy-looking domestic moggie, displaying a psychedelic dyed pattern in his fur in the form of shooting stars and planets.

'Maybe so,' continued Millicent; 'however, I have discovered a much more insidious and lethal crop being cultivated in a secret location in the foothills, of such proportions that, if discovered, it is sure to visit unwanted attention on our area.' She paused again for effect.

'Cocaine, fellow felines! Cocaine and the production of amphetamines!' she announced, rising dramatically to stand on her back legs with front paws extended. 'And in such commercial quantities that it is obvious it is being produced for enormous profits by unscrupulous criminals for distribution in the cities. The discovery of this would, of course, bring our existence into disrepute and could bring an end to our peaceful and peace-loving way of life.'

There was a general uproar from the congregation with further cat-calls of denial and disbelief from certain members of the group. Others looked silently at their neighbours in consternation.

'Where is this location?' called one.

'It must be destroyed immediately,' said another fearfully.

'We can't afford to be investigated,' said another. 'Further media attention and constant spying and raids will destroy our lifestyle!'

'Exactly!' called Millicent over the uproar. 'Neighbour against neighbour, friend against friend! We mustn't allow it!' Her voice rose to a crescendo, 'And furthermore there is also a suspicion that the recent demise of the town's vet is in some way connected to this dangerous and destructive enterprise!'

There was a gasp of disbelief and an elderly domesticated tabby matron called out, 'What can we do? We're only cats.'

'Well,' replied Millicent in a quieter, more reasonable tone, 'quite by accident I have discovered that the level of acidic content of some of our colleagues' urine is highly destructive to certain plants, such as hemp or cannabis and, I suspect, possibly the coca plant. Bertha has told me that your social club ranks are made up of sufferers of this particular condition and I suggest we can use this to our advantage.'

There was a mystified silence and Millicent continued. 'I am asking all of you to fill your bladders to overflowing and join Bertha and me on a raid of the coca crop and spray it into oblivion. I cannot assure you that we will be successful but for the sake of our town I believe it is worth a try. – Are you with us?'

There was a long silence and Millicent was beginning to think her plea had fallen on deaf ears when suddenly a roar of approval erupted from the audience.

'Let's do it!' they screamed. 'Let's flood the place with piss!'

'Thank you, my friends,' Millicent cried gratefully. 'I knew I could rely on you. I propose we form an action committee to organise the time and meeting place and other logistics and I suggest we all meet again at a time to be decided. Bertha will be in contact with your social committee in the very near future with instructions for the raid.' She paused and looked out into the gathering, enthusiastically. 'Thank you all once again for your co-operation and dedication in keeping Nimbin and its surrounds safe and secure for the feline population and for the generations that will follow.'

There was a resounding response as Millicent made her way back into the crowd. Marcel sidled up to her through the appreciative throng. 'Well done, Millicent. May I have a quiet word with you somewhere?'

Flushed with her success, she nodded and led the way out through the entrance into the cool night air. They settled on a little hillock overlooking a field of cultivated proteas, waratah and flannel flowers, and their slight perfume pervaded the air.

'Well, you certainly got your message across to them,' Marcel said as he settled down on his haunches, 'but do you honestly think it will work? I mean, there seem to be quite a few acid urine contenders but I think it may take an extensive army of pissers to poison a commercial crop of coca plants.'

'Oh, we won't be able to cover the whole crop in one sitting, so to speak,' Millicent replied, 'but we could make a sizeable inroad. It probably will take regular attacks before we get a result but at least we'll be making an attempt – maybe even a statement.'

Marcel smiled. 'I must say I admire your determination.'

'I had thought of setting fire to it but that has its problems,' Millicent conceded. 'For a start we're not really equipped for striking matches and even if we could set it alight, there's always the danger of starting a bushfire and that could be disastrous to the entire area.'

'Why don't you call in the big guns from down south?' he said feigning innocence. 'They could send in choppers loaded with weed killer and wipe out the whole crop in one mission.'

Startled, Millicent looked at him in surprise. 'Choppers – from down south? What on earth are you talking about?'

He turned to face her, dropping his voice to a confidential whisper. 'We have a mutual friend I believe – Tom, from Canberra.'

Millicent looked at him aghast. 'Tom? You're one of us?'

Marcel nodded. 'I've been sent out here to give you a bit of back-up. Hasn't Tom notified you?'

'Well, I haven't been able to check my emails for a day or two; what with arranging tonight's meeting, and every time I go into the office, Pat or Jenny – they're my staff,' she explained, 'have been online themselves.'

'I was stationed in Lismore when I was advised,' Marcel explained. 'They're sending in a new vet to replace Dr Fellini but he'll only be a casual until they work out a more suitable arrangement.'

'But what about King?' Millicent blurted out before she could control her response. 'Will he remain on the assignment?'

'King?' Marcel pondered the question.

'He's FBI. – A Burmese. – He worked with Fellini. I sent that information to Tom. He was going to check up on the protocol.'

'Ah, yes,' replied Marcel. 'Well, there seems to be a bit of a problem there. You see, the FBI are playing it very cool as usual and not giving anything away. They're not even admitting to having an agent in the area.'

'Typical,' muttered Millicent.

'Tom wants us to carry on as a team and leave King out of the loop until he gets confirmation.'

'But we've been working on this together,' Millicent responded heatedly. 'He was very close to Fellini. I can't just ignore his contribution.'

'Just keep it on a "need to know" basis until we hear from headquarters,' said Marcel.

'Oh, why can't the Intelligence Agencies get their act together?' Millicent lamented.

Marcel shrugged his shoulders and began to groom his lustrous, ginger fur.

They returned to the raging party, which the evening had turned into. Bertha's hash-mouse cookies had been a huge success and the guests were in high spirits. Marcel and Millicent danced to a reggae cat band and Millicent found herself becoming more and more attracted to the ginger tom from Lismore. But she quickly realised the danger in becoming attached to a fellow agent and made her excuses to leave. Bertha was really away with the pixies, rapping away and extemporising really bad hip-hop lyrics, rolling around on the ground, kicking up her paws and laughing hysterically, so Millicent made her way home alone.

Chapter 14

No sooner had she arrived on the back verandah than King suddenly appeared. He was still obviously distraught and Millicent tried to console him but to no avail.

'My informant at the police station has told me the police are interviewing all of the clients on the surgery's records. It appears Mr Delmonte has an alibi. He was supposedly home all night. It was backed up by Bruce, the cook and the daughter,' he said bitterly, 'as if they'd be reliable witnesses.'

'So it seems like we have to look elsewhere,' said Millicent. 'Maybe we should start with Dr Fellini's corsage of concubines.'

'But I *know* Victor Delmonte was responsible for his death,' King growled in frustration as he paced the verandah. 'They had obviously been arguing on the night of his death and Delmonte actually warned him he wouldn't be blackmailed and to keep his nose out of his business.'

'Blackmailed?' Millicent asked, surprised. 'You never mentioned that. Why would he think he was being blackmailed?'

'Fellini had threatened to go to the authorities and ask them to check Delmonte's drug trade background,' King reluctantly admitted. 'He was advising Delmonte to get out of the area while he still could.'

'Why would Fellini show his hand like that? Why would he warn him he was under investigation?'

King shrugged. 'Because there's no actual evidence of Delmonte's involvement in any drug trade, I suppose, and he wanted him out of the area. I know Delmonte is a very ruthless, vindictive character.'

'But Dr Fellini drove me home and Delmonte was still at his mansion. And I'm sure no one followed us. I'm trained to notice things like that.'

'But what about later?' replied King. 'He could've sent that gun-happy moron Bruce to take care of him.'

'Then why wasn't Fellini shot? That would've been the logical way for Bruce to respond.'

'Maybe Delmonte gave instructions to make it look like a suicide.'

'Then why remove all his clothes?' asked Millicent. 'That just doesn't make sense.'

'You just don't know what was involved,' mumbled King, sinking to the floor despondently.

'Just what *was* involved, King?' asked Millicent.

King sighed hopelessly. 'This was to be our last case,' he said. 'We were going to retire to the Gold Coast. Fellini was getting past his prime as an agent. He had his problems.' There was a long uncomfortable pause before he continued reluctantly, 'I think Fellini may have been blackmailing him – for money – for his retirement.'

Millicent looked at him steadfastly and then asked, 'King, did he know about the cocaine?'

He avoided her eye contact as cats do, but dropped his head in shame.

'Yes,' he replied softly. 'But,' lifting his head as if to justify his partner's behaviour, 'he didn't know about the plantation, I swear. We didn't know where it was coming from. We were getting close to finding out but Delmonte got to him first.'

'I see, a bent agent,' said Millicent noncommittally. 'But surely the FBI will send a replacement to work with you; they've lost one of their agents.'

King shook his head. 'After it was discovered I was working with a compromised agent? I don't think so. *I'd* be compromised. At best I'd have to be recalled and retrained with another agent. No, it would be easier to leave me out in the cold and send another couple of agents to take our place. My barcode is past swiping, Princess,' he sighed, lying down on the deck.

Millicent couldn't help but feel sorry for this once-dashing Burmese agent who it now appeared had no future. She lay down beside him and cuddled into his back.

Suddenly she remembered the emails she was expecting from Tom, got up, and made her way into the office. Pat and Jenny were obviously sleeping and the computer was booted up and ready to go. She quickly connected to the web and downloaded the messages. Of course there were none from Tom in the inbox as Pat or Jenny would've deleted them. She went into the deleted file and quickly found what she was looking for.

There were some instructions and an attachment that was simply titled 'mug shots'. She downloaded the pictures and the resulting images puzzled her. She thought she recognised one of the men but for the life of her, she couldn't remember where she'd seen him. The inscription beneath the picture read '*Robert Lyons AKA Victor Delmonte, Vince Da Virtuoso, Sol Da Sniffer and several other aliases – suspected drug trafficker – whereabouts unknown – considered of interest to the drug enforcement agency. Possibly deceased. No definitive proof available.*'

Beneath that Tom had added the altered lyrics of an old World War 1 ballad: '*There's apparently a long white trail a'winding beyond the land of his dreams.*'

In another email Tom reported that the area where the coca plantation was situated was in the name of a company. He was checking out the directors but there didn't appear to be any connection with any of Delmonte's aliases at this stage. The investigation was ongoing.

Millicent hurried out to tell King what she'd discovered but he was asleep. No wonder, she thought as she looked at him, he must be exhausted. She was about to rouse him when Bertha suddenly arrived home and staggered up the stairs propped up by Marcel.

'I thought she might need a bit of assistance.' Marcel grinned like a Cheshire. 'She's really out of it and feeling no pain.'

'So it seems. I take it she had her share of the supper?' Millicent remarked in amusement.

'Her share and several others,' replied Marcel, smiling.

Bertha drew herself up in a dignified attempt to regain her composure, looking like some English dowager duchess. 'I'll have you know, I am well in control of my facilities,' she said very slowly and with the hint of a slur, and headed for her basket in the corner. Unfortunately her head was held so high she failed to notice King lying in front of her and tripped over him, finishing up splayed out like a drunken rat catcher. King jumped up preparing to protect himself from attack and came face to face with Marcel. They arched their backs, bristled their fur, and hissed of course. Millicent sighed, resigned to this inevitable display of tomcat testosterone.

'Okay, boys, cool it,' she said, 'we've got things to discuss.'

'So you must be King,' Marcel said, sidling up to the Burmese and sniffing sedately. 'I'm Marcel – I'm only new in town. I'm an old friend of Millicent's.'

'Friend?' replied King suspiciously. 'Or do you mean partner?'

Marcel flicked his green eyes at Millicent, questioningly.

Millicent nodded and said, 'Oh, alright,' and squatted on her haunches. 'Yes, he's my new partner.' Turning her head to Marcel, she said, 'King is FBI, and, in the typical fashion of our respective agencies with their *independent agendas* and lack of intelligence sharing, we've been sent on the same assignment.' She paused and softened her tone. 'King's partner, Dr Fellini, the local vet, died recently under suspicious circumstances. Naturally, he's a little upset.'

'I see,' said Marcel. 'Sorry, old man, I guess we've all been through that at one time or another.'

'We'd been together since I graduated from the Academy,' said King. 'I want revenge – I want Delmonte.'

Millicent quickly filled Marcel in on the suspected Delmonte association and then turned back to King.

'It's not just revenge we're after, King,' Millicent said gently. 'We have other priorities. Our mission is to close down the drug trade in the area and bring the perpetrators to justice. If Fellini's murder means so much to you, then you concentrate on that and Marcel and I will get on with our assignment.'

'I don't know, Millicent,' said Marcel. 'This Delmonte character does sound suspicious and I suppose we could investigate any possible murder connection at the same time. After all, Fellini was a fellow agent and there are three of us now so we can cover a lot of ground.'

King looked at him gratefully but, still considering himself the alpha male, he felt forced to bluster, 'Don't bother, I'm quite capable of running my own investigation. I'm hardly a rookie.'

For the sake of peace, Millicent reluctantly acquiesced to the domineering male ego. 'Oh, alright,' she said, 'and at the top of the list of murder suspects I suggest we place the floral femmes: Freesia from the bakery, Poppy from the craft shop and Lilly from the library. King, we'll leave it to you to discover the glass blower. Injecting poison into the victim is a common female method so maybe we should start there.'

The two toms nodded in agreement.

'Now,' said Millicent taking charge, 'I'm in the process of instigating a raid on the coca plantation and I'm going to need all the co-operation I can get.' She turned to the two conspirators. 'It's going to be tricky but I think we can pull it off.'

She laid out her plan as the two toms listened, each adding their contribution to the detail. At the end, she sat back, wiped her snout with a paw and said, 'Well, what do you think?'

Marcel and King looked at each other, considering the possibilities and then nodded.

'Sounds good. But first,' said Marcel, 'we have to establish the definite identity of the suspect.'

'Right,' agreed Millicent. 'I intend to revisit the Delmonte property tomorrow night and try to get a look at this Mr Delmonte. My control sent me a copy of the mug shot of the suspect but getting a good look at him could be a problem. He obviously keeps a low profile.'

'Why don't I come along with you, Milly – sorry, Millicent?' King said. 'After all I seemed to get on quite well with the daughter. I mean, I did sleep in her bed,' he added with a provocative smile.

'And Bruce also tried to blow you away,' replied Millicent, pointedly. 'And don't forget the Rottweilers.'

'Perhaps the three of us should go,' suggested Marcel. 'We could watch each other's backs and maybe be able to distract their attention.'

'Agency co-operation?' Millicent smiled wryly. 'This'll be a first.'

'I think it would be better to go during the daylight,' said Marcel. 'There's a better chance this Delmonte character may be out and about.'

'But what about the dogs?' asked Millicent.

'Leave the dogs to me,' said King. 'Being fore-warned gives us a definite advantage. Now, can we get a look at this mug shot?'

Millicent slipped inside and found the coast clear. Pat and Jenny were still sleeping so the computer was free. She retraced her steps and gestured for King and Marcel to follow her. She quickly downloaded the picture and printed a couple of copies. Marcel gently pushed the office door almost closed in case the sound of the elderly printer woke Pat and Jenny. Then, taking a copy each in their teeth, they stole back out onto the verandah.

'Oooooh, Tarquin,' Bertha mumbled in her sleep, 'not again. You sailor boys are insatiable.'

The next morning, the three 'mouseketeers' rendezvoused at a spot close to their objective.

'My God,' exclaimed Marcel to an unusually plump-looking King, 'did you go on a feeding frenzy last night or are you pregnant?'

Millicent giggled. 'Oh, I forgot to tell you, Marcel, King is a sort of prototype secret weapon. He's had plastic surgery which gave him a pouch and independent movement of his front digits.'

'What?' Marcel exclaimed in disbelief. 'Well, wouldn't ya know the FBI would think of something as grotesque as that!' he said in disgust. 'They may as well have just trained a wallaby.'

'Wallabies don't have the same high IQ,' retorted King loftily. 'Now,' he said, unzipping his pouch, 'you wait here and I'll deal with the dogs.'

Sniffing the air he soon picked up the scent of the dogs and crept forward slowly, using all the available cover. Randy and Rodney were lying in a ditch they'd obviously scratched out of the earth. The old gardener was raking up leaves and dead weeds he'd obviously been digging out of the garden.

King surreptitiously slipped a paw into his pouch and removed a few small pieces of beef he'd managed to steal from the local butcher. He kicked the meat towards the two dozing dogs. The sudden movement and sound of the meat hitting the ground woke Randy and Rodney and they jumped to their feet, immediately on guard, sniffing the air for an intruder. King crouched low, concealed by the prolifically blooming, mock orange bush he had chosen as a hiding place. But the overpowering smell of the meat was the only odour the guard dogs detected and they cautiously crept forward to investigate. Discovering the meat they set about salivating, chomping and gulping it down with great delight.

Within a few minutes the Percocet that King had retrieved from his hidden stash of drugs took effect. The two dogs began to wobble on their legs, staggering around like hounds on hashish or mutts on mescalin until they finally dropped to the ground and fell asleep without a care in the world. The old gardener continued raking, oblivious to the state of his drugged protectors.

King crept back to his co-conspirators and gave them the all-clear signal and the trio began their exploration. As they passed the now sleeping dogs, Millicent glanced in the direction of the gardener who turned to pick up a pile of leaves he had gathered. As he stood up Millicent suddenly gasped.

'That's him!' she whispered excitedly. 'The gardener! That's Victor Delmonte! We've found him! I knew I'd seen him before – at the markets! He was with a beautiful young woman and they drove off with another man in an expensive SUV! Delmonte was dressed in a shabby second-hand outfit. That's why people don't recognise him. He just looks like a hundred other deadbeat hippies.'

They crouched low to the ground and King again fiddled with his pouch and produced a small digital camera. He lined up a close-up of Delmonte and clicked off several shots.

'Dad,' called a young woman's voice from behind them, 'morning tea is ready. Where do you want it?'

Millicent swung around to the direction from which she'd heard the female voice. 'And that's the beautiful young woman who was with him!' she exclaimed.

'That's the lovely daughter, Amethyst,' King acknowledged. 'Amy.'

'Coming,' the old man replied.

The young woman approached and, seeing the three cats, stopped and exclaimed, 'King, is that you? You're back! Where on earth did you get to the other night? And you've brought some friends,' she cried, delighted.

King quickly returned the camera to his pouch and zipped it up. To distract Amy's attention, Millicent walked sedately towards her in her best catwalk style.

'Oh,' said Amy, 'what an exotic little pussy you are!' Millicent preened and purred and Amy bent to pick her up. 'And what's your name, my little beauty?' She looked for a name on Millicent's collar. 'Millicent,' Amy read with obvious approval. 'And where do you come from, Millicent, hmmm?' Millicent purred even louder as Amy stroked her ears and head.

'Bloody stray cats,' her father growled as he approached. 'A lot of good these two mongrels are,' referring to Randy and Rodney. 'Look at them, fast asleep.'

'You three better get off home,' said Amy, as she gently put Millicent back on the ground. 'If Randy and Rodney wake up and see you there'll be hell to pay.' She gave King a quick stroke and tickle on his ear.

Marcel wandered off, slightly offended that he had been ignored.

'Yeah, that bastard Fellini won't be able to help you this time,' the old man chortled. 'In fact he ain't gonna be helping anyone anymore.'

To Millicent's surprise, Amy joined in her father's mirth as the father and daughter made off towards the house. 'And he ain't gonna try and blackmail me anymore neither, is he, darlin'?' he continued as they headed for a paved courtyard where Amy had laid out the morning refreshments.

'Well, Dad, when an animal goes feral you just have to put him down, don't you?' she giggled. 'It's more humane.'

The three Agents shared a conspiratorial look and headed towards the front entrance, their infiltration into enemy territory completely successful.

'I think we can forget about investigating Fellini's *leis,*' said Millicent. 'From that little exchange, Delmonte is the prime suspect for the murder *and* the drugs, in my opinion.'

'But it wasn't the old man who murdered my partner,' said King. 'It was his daughter, Amy. She was wearing the same perfume today that I smelt in the surgery on the morning after he was murdered.' Millicent and Marcel stopped and stared at King. 'She must've come into town later that night, seduced him in the surgery and injected him,' he said.

'From his reputation, I don't think that would've been too hard. I wonder if it was before or after he'd injected her,' replied Millicent dryly. 'So her name is actually Amethyst,' she added thoughtfully. 'It seems your ex-partner was switching from flowers to gem stones.'

Chapter 15

Despite their reservations, King and Marcel accompanied Millicent and Bertha to the agreed meeting spot at an old abandoned farmhouse, where they were amazed to find an army of other cats waiting for them. The mix of ages, breeds and colours was a sight to behold: some were tawny, tabby and tattered; some were black and white and wily; some grey, grizzled and disgruntled; and others were inbred and insignificant; but all were committed and determined.

It was a dark, overcast night with just a hint of an easterly breeze as they formed into ragged ranks and followed Millicent across the countryside to the coca plantation. At the barbed wire fence bordering the dark and daunting undergrowth, she gave them all a final warning and repeated her instructions to ensure everyone was clear on their designated deployment.

The first stop was the stream that ran through the property so the troops could refresh and refill their bladders, and then it was on to their objectives. Some acted as lookouts for any sign of the vicious guard dogs that Millicent and King had warned them of and all had sharpened their claws in preparation for combat. It had been decided on a three-point assault on the crops: one to the front and one on each flank. The army advanced.

Silently the troops slipped through the bush, some camouflaged with twigs and leaves and some relying on their mottled colours. They found the hidden plantation not far from the laboratory. Soon dozens of tails were raised for action. Millicent gave the signal using her reflective diamante collar and the attack began. Litres of urine were sprayed onto the coca plantation, the combined gushing sound reminiscent of Niagara Falls filling the night. As bladders were depleted, the backup troops stepped in and took their place and the first wave retreated back to the stream for more ammunition.

The noise of the bombardment alerted the guard dogs who ran to counter-attack and defend their territory, barking and growling ferociously.

'My God, they've brought in reinforcements!' Millicent yelled as she saw a pack of Dobermans and Pit Bulls join the Rottweilers in a savage attack. The wave of feline lookouts moved in, slashing and clawing at the unprotected noses of the enemy. Cat bodies were shaken and thrown into the air only to land on their feet on another defender, with extended claws and teeth sinking into the backs of the foe. The whimpering and cries of the wounded mixed with the growling, yelping, squawking and caterwauling of combat.

This, of course, alerted the human members of the gang who immediately realised they were under siege and grabbed for their rifles to defend themselves. They burst forth from the laboratory and ran through the disguised entrance into the plantation, with guns raised and firing indiscriminately. The carnage was horrendous.

Parked beside the laboratory was the Delmontes' SUV and Victor and his daughter had just arrived in time to witness the battle. They ran into the lab to protect their investment, shouting orders to their roughneck associates to wipe out the intruders.

'Crikey!' shouted Victor. 'It looks like a mass escape from the local cat refuge! It reminds me of the Nowra breakout of World War 2!'

Millicent quickly ascertained the deployment of the pack of guard dogs and from her position high in a Eucalyptus, sounded the retreat, but the sounds of battle drowned out the warning. King, narrowly avoiding the snapping jaws of a Bull Terrier, ran into the fray shouting, 'Retreat! Retreat!' as Marcel fought off a Doberman who had grabbed Bertha's tail mid-squirt. Marcel clung on tenaciously as the dog yelped and shook his head, trying to throw him off.

'Get back, Bertha!' cried Marcel, as he disappeared into the throng. 'Tell the troops to retreat! We must survive to fight another day!'

King withdrew a cigarette lighter from his pouch and with his scientifically developed dextrous digits flicked it alight. He bent and touched the jet of flame to a heap of dried grass which immediately burst into a ball of flame and began to spread rapidly.

Above the sounds of gunshots, yelling, growling and yelping, Millicent suddenly heard the welcome sound of a helicopter approaching at speed. She looked up and smiled. A model crop duster chopper appeared out of the night skies heading for the plantation, the fire which King had started making an excellent target signal. The chopper dived, flying low over the crop, releasing its payload. The weedkiller drifted to the ground, settling onto the coca plants. Victor and Amy ran to the entrance of the building with Victor screaming, 'The chopper! Get the chopper!'

The gang immediately turned its attention to the helicopter and began firing. The crop duster made a second pass and just as it finished the run a fusillade of bullets hit it as it banked. The motor coughed and spluttered and smoke began to pour from its engine. The rotors began to slow and the chopper began to fall. Suddenly a parachute ejected from the doomed aircraft and began to flutter downward in the wind.

'Thank God,' Millicent sighed in relief. 'Butch lives to fly another day.'

She continued to watch as the chopper dropped from the sky, crashed directly onto the laboratory and exploded like an incendiary bomb. The horrendous explosion obviously caused by explosives and ammunition stored in the building for land clearing, dam building and emergency defence purposes completely destroyed the building, its contents and the surrounds in a ball of flames.

Millicent smiled to herself. It was always good to have a backup plan.

King joined her at the base of the Eucalyptus tree. 'Well, I guess that settles the score for Dr Fellini,' he said. 'Both of the Delmontes were inside. They went up with the laboratory, I'm pleased to say.'

'And you got your revenge,' Millicent smiled affectionately.

'And you completed your assignment,' King smiled back.

'We *both* completed our assignment,' Millicent reminded him.

'You know,' said King, with a glint in his eye, 'we make a pretty good team.'

'And I suppose I didn't contribute anything,' Marcel said, as he limped towards them.

'Oh, you're hurt, Marcel,' Millicent said, hurrying to him in concern.

'Just a scratch or two,' replied Marcel with a wry grin, 'nothing that a couple of Bertha's hash-mouse cookies won't repair.'

They all laughed and rubbed up against each other, purring.

The police and fire brigade arrived at the scene soon after, of course, and found the place deserted. The remaining gang members had fled but left enough evidence to close the case of the mysterious Delmonte debacle. But even with the fire that destroyed the coca crop and lab extinguished, they still had to wear their respirators to contend with the overpowering smell of cat's pee.

The surviving Pee-hew Social Club members staggered back to their abodes in the surrounding farms, homes and properties, dragging the wounded but with a new-found sense of self-esteem. Bertha, even more tattered than she had been prior to the battle, had also discovered a new sense of fulfilment. She would never again relieve herself on Reg and his sons' cannabis plants next door, but she would manage to keep their mouse population and consequently her aches and pains under control.

Later, Millicent, King and Marcel rested on the back verandah. 'Well, it looks like a successful outcome to our assignment,' purred Millicent. 'Thanks, guys.'

Marcel yawned. 'Yep,' he said. 'I suppose its back to Lismore for me. Pity; we don't get much excitement like this around the Northern Rivers. What about you, King? I suppose you'll be recalled to Sydney?'

King completed grooming himself and sighed. 'I suppose so,' he said. 'I guess I'll have to train another operative and off we'll go again to foreign parts. The war goes on.'

Suddenly they heard Bertha's voice coming around the side of the house. 'No, I'm sure Pat and Jenny won't mind. They're real cat lovers. Oh, and I must take you over to the farm next door, too. They've got a plague of the most delicious mice over there.' She appeared around the corner in excited conversation with another cat, a rough-looking, well-built domesticated tabby who looked a bit the worse for wear. His fur was singed, he was limping and wearing a ripped and battered leather flying helmet.

'Butch!' Millicent exclaimed, getting to her feet and rushing toward him. 'Thank God you survived! I saw your chute open but then I lost sight of you. Are you alright?'

'I'm just fine, Ms Millicent,' said Butch. 'I was staggering around lost in the bush when this lovely young lady found me and offered to help.'

King and Marcel shared an amazed look at the 'lovely young lady' remark but wisely kept their own counsel.

'Butch was the helicopter pilot,' remarked Millicent to the two other toms. 'He was a part of the back-up plan.'

'What back-up plan?' asked King.

'Well,' Millicent said, 'I wasn't all that confident that the acid piss plan would work so I arranged with Tom to send in the heavy artillery just to make sure. I didn't think we'd get another opportunity.' She turned to Butch. 'Did they get the chance to test the sample I sent, Butch?'

Butch smiled. 'They certainly did. What do you think I was spraying out there tonight?'

'Bertha, you're a heroine!' cried Millicent.

'Me?' replied Bertha in disbelief. 'Why?'

'Tell her, Butch,' smiled Millicent.

'Well, Ms Millicent sent down a sample of your – er – urine and it was passed on to the CSIRO lab for research.'

'That's Cats Scientific Investigation Research Organisation,' Millicent interjected.

'It was given top priority,' Butch continued, 'and they came up with a chemical equivalent plus a few additives that would do the same job. They've called it Agent Pink, and that's what I sprayed over the coca plantation tonight. It's a selective weed killer that won't damage the ecology or do permanent damage to the soil. It will kill off any plant with a trace of THC but it won't affect any other growth. It can also be seeded with viable crops to suit an area for profitable regrowth. It's going to come in quite handy when they send it over to the Golden Triangle.'

'Oh, my,' exclaimed Bertha, in amazement, 'and I just thought I had a simple medical condition. I could be the saviour of the Third World countries!'

The others burst out laughing but were suddenly stilled by the kitchen light being switched on and Pat's voice calling, 'Who's out there? Hello, is there anyone there?'

She opened the back door and stepped out into the early light of the dawn. 'Hell, what's this, a bloody cat refuge?' she exclaimed. 'Where did you lot come from?'

King, Marcel and Butch took off in a rush and disappeared around the corner of the house.

'Have you two tarts been entertaining?' asked Pat with a smile on her face. She bent down and picked up the empty food bowls. 'Well, I guess you're ready for breakfast, eh?'

She disappeared back into the kitchen and Millicent and Bertha could hear the clatter of dried vegetarian cat biscuits hitting the plastic bowls. They took off at great speed after King, Marcel and Butch.

Chapter 16

At the prearranged pick-up area in the bush, miles from town, they waited for the helicopter to descend. The door slid open and, to their surprise, out stepped the debonair Tom to meet them. Millicent, Marcel and Butch rushed over to greet him. King held back, watchfully.

'Hi guys,' said the smiling chief of operations for the CIA. 'I hope you're honoured, I flew this thing all the way from Canberra to pick you chaps up. Thanks for the mayday call, Butch; that made it all much simpler.' He acknowledged Millicent and Marcel with a respectful nod, turned back to Butch and said, 'I think you deserve a bit of a vacation, Butch, just until you get yourself back into shape again, eh?'

Butch grinned in appreciation and turned back to the edge of the clearing. There, a forlorn Bertha sat upright with a small tear trickling from her one good eye down into her sparse whiskers. Her tattered paw was raised in farewell.

'Thank you, chief, there just happens to be a little lady over there who's offered to nurse me back to health,' he said.

'Well, I see you haven't lost it, Butch,' Tom smiled. 'Go for it, old man.'

With farewell smiles and twitching tails, Millicent, King and Marcel boarded the helicopter, with Tom taking the pilot's seat. The chopper blades roared into life and the aircraft rose majestically into the clear blue sky.

Millicent sat between her two new friends, the illustrious King, with his mesmerising, golden eyes, and the easygoing, attractive ginger, Marcel. She looked out the window and smiled as they banked over the statuesque Nimbin Rocks and the rolling Nightcap Ranges. The countryside looked so beautiful with its intense foliage, vibrant green paddocks dotted with feeding cattle, and the creeks and waterfalls glistening in the early morning sun.

I'm going to miss this place, she thought as her memory flashed a montage of images of the colourful village, its friendly relaxed people and the friends she had made, the peace and the excitement she had experienced. It's such a beautiful world, she mused, philosophically, if only the stupid humans weren't determined to stuff it up.

Her wistful thoughts were interrupted by Tom's voice, raised above the sound of the engine. 'Well, team, good work, well done. In fact, so well done, there's serious talk about forming a new division and you three have been nominated to head the team.'

The three agents looked at each other incredulously.

'But I'm with the FBI,' said King, smiling dubiously. 'I don't think they'll be entirely agreeable to losing one of their operatives to another Agency.'

Tom smiled. 'I've been in touch with your superiors and after the usual long drawn-out discussions; we've finally agreed that, if you're willing, having one of their top agents involved may open new doors of cooperation between the intelligence-gathering organisations.'

The proposed team stared at each other in amazement.

'And what's this new division to be called?' asked Millicent.

'ASIO,' replied Tom, with a twinkle in his eyes, 'the Australian Shorthair Intelligence Organisation.'

Epilogue

On the back deck, Jenny lay comfortably stretched out on an outdoor recliner taking advantage of the cool breeze blowing gently from the south. On her lap, she lightly stroked Butch who was curled up and purring contentedly. I think I've died and gone to heaven, he thought: lovely new carers, a lovely new home in a lovely new location with a lovely new girlfriend. This is definitely what I call retirement.

Bertha lay languidly stretched out on the deck watching him. What a hunk, she thought; he reminds me so much of Tarquin. And I thought I was past it! She sighed in satisfaction.

Pat suddenly came out the back door in high excitement. 'Jen, you won't believe it but I was just checking the emails and we got one from someone called Tom at the Kittyhawk Animal Refuge!'

Jenny stirred and looked at her quizzically. 'Kittyhawk Animal Refuge? Never heard of it.'

'Me neither, but they found Millicent! Tom said some people picked her up and thought she was a stray so they took her to the refuge. The refuge checked her microchip and linked it up with Dr Fellini's inquiry and got in touch with Mr Scratchpole in Canberra. He'd obviously been travelling overseas and had just got back. Well, he told them who he'd sold Millicent to and the refuge was able to get in touch with the young couple in Blue Knob and sent her back there.'

'Well,' said Jenny, hugely relieved, 'thank God she's safe. I was so worried about her.'

'It appears that the couple asked the refuge people to get in touch with us and thank us for taking such good care of

Millicent. They said she was in excellent condition, more beautiful than ever, and they'd missed her so much. Dr Fellini must've left our details with the microchip registration mob.'

'Oh, that was nice of them,' said Jenny. 'Well, as long as she's happy and back with people who love her. Bertha's got a new friend so she's got company and I swear she's much more sprightly than she was before Millicent, and certainly before Butch, arrived.'

Jenny lifted Butch off her lap, carefully placed him on the deck near Bertha, and rose from the recliner. 'Let me have a look at the email,' she said as she made her way inside with Pat. 'You see? God looks after all the animals, great and small,' she continued as they disappeared from sight.

'So does the Agency, apparently,' mewed Butch, winking at Bertha, who seductively rolled over on her back and smiled back up at him.

Bryon Williams, ex-stage and television actor, script writer, producer, director turned novelist, has now retired to a Retirement Village in Brisbane. Two of his previous novels, *The Grumpy Old Withered of Oz*, a comedic, semi-autobiographical book about the frustrations of ageing and life as his wife's carer in the not-so-fast lane of the Zzzzzzzzz Generation, and *The Twilight Escort Agency*, an hilarious and bawdy account of a mythical escort agency for the 'more mature' client, have enjoyed very positive independent reader response, as has this novel, the whimsical comedy crime-fantasy, ideal for cat lovers, *Code Name: Millicent – The Cat Intelligence Agent Who Came Out of the Cold*.

Tourist from the Light, an intriguing paranormal romance with an underlying theme of a thought-provoking alternative spiritual philosophy, followed. His fifth novel, *The Burning Boy*, is an exciting action/crime page-turner based on the horrors that haunt an ex-Vietnam War cameraman who returns to Australia in the mid seventies and becomes inadvertently involved in a sophisticated and lethal people-smuggling racket.

Bryon's beloved wife of 45 years, Marie, suffered a disastrous stroke in 2000 and he retired to become her full-time carer until she passed on in 2014. Bryon went on to write a memoir of his career and his married life, *A Light at the End*, which received numerous 5-star favourable reviews.

With the legalisation of gay marriage and acceptance of sexual equality, Bryon then changed course and wrote *Naked Warrior*, a gay, erotic love story based on Bryon's belief in Reincarnation.

Intrigued and inspired by an old friend's unresolved story of the tragic murder of her daughter in 1988, they collaborated to co-write *Not in the Public Interest*, published in 2019.

CPSIA information can be obtained
at www.ICGtesting.com
Printed in the USA
LVHW011734040820
662391LV00013B/1257